The Lost Inheritance Mystery

by
BEN HAMMOTT

The Lost Inheritance Mystery

Ben Hammott

Cover Design by Keith Draws

Note from Author

First of all, I would like you, the reader, to know that every single sale of one of my books gives me a thrill. That you have taken a chance on a relatively unknown author, (you brave adventurous soul,) and are willing to invest your time and money in something I have created, is an act I am most humbly grateful for.

What you are about to read is a humorous mystery thriller set in early 1900, which revolves around the search for a lost inheritance of vast wealth. H hope you enjoy the story and my English sense of humour.

Lastly, as with all new authors starting out on this adventure into the literary world, we do appreciate your comments and any reviews you may feel inspired to write. Please feel free to contact me with any comments you might have about the book via this email address: **benhammott@gmail.com**

That's it, all finished, except to say, THANK YOU and I hope your time spent reading this book will prove to be an enjoyable experience.

Ben Hammott

BLIND PIRATE
TAVERN

London, December, 1922

The **thief, who** liked to be known as *Furtive Freddy,* but, much to his dismay, was commonly addressed by those who had the displeasure of his acquaintance as *Foul Freddy*—the reason for which will soon become apparent—shunned the preferred dark colours of his shady profession. Vanity was to blame for his frowned upon decision. His chosen burglary profession was a night-time activity that left the days free for sleeping and Furtive and the sun total strangers. The result was his complexion had taken on a corpselike tone that he thought too much black accentuated. Due to this reason and his total lack of style and colour coordination, Furtive wore a green long-tailed coat over a gold patterned waistcoat, a collarless light-blue striped shirt, brown and orange checked baggy trousers and a bright red neckerchief. The only black he conceded to wear were his boots, a crumpled top hat worn slightly at an angle, and the years of accumulated dirt stored under his fingernails.

Oblivious to his shortcomings, his eyes scanned the large old manor house emerging from the wispy mist that veiled the wild overgrown gardens, now more weed than bloom, and the fifty yards of scrub grass that concealed all memory of the once admired manicured lawn he would have to cross to reach it. Lit by the gloomy light of a typical English nightfall, the burglar took in its architectural features. Wooden steps led up to a veranda edged with railings that wrapped around two sides of the house; wooden columns set at intervals along the railing supported its dipped and sagging roof. At three stories high with sharply angled slate roofs, the highest feature was a tall central tower with a small round window peering over the landscape like an all seeing-eye. It must at one time been a grand and impressive building. That time was long ago, possibly even before the man about to force his entry inside was born. The burglar received the impression of a habitation falling into senility, tired of its centuries of existence. Just like people, houses age, and though the process is slower, it is no less unavoidable; in both, decay is hastened by reasons other than the passage of the ticking clock. Lack of regular maintenance had caused the old manor house to age more speedily than it otherwise might have. The person responsible? Its current owner, Ebenezer Drooge. A man proud of his miserly personality and his name, which he believed had been inspired by a distant relation to that of Dickens's penny-pinching character.

Furtive's eyes rested on the single lit window seeping candlelight into the darkness. While he waited for it to be extinguished, his mind travelled back to the events that had brought him to this neglected house.

Two weeks before he had been quietly sipping a beer in his favourite drinking hole, the *Blind Pirate Tavern*, one of the few drinking establishments that would still let him enter, when the door opened. Furtive was alerted to the opening by the cold breeze whooshing up his baggy trouser legs, and the stench of filthy streets tainted with odours best left unimagined that clawed its way inside and promptly assaulted every nostril in the inn. Furtive tilted his head slightly to bring his furtive gaze upon the person who had entered. He saw a man ill at odds with his surroundings. That he did not belong here was as obvious as a wounded haddock in a shark tank, though in this scenario, the haddock had a better chance of survival. Furtive watched the man with interest to see what would unfold.

The name of the 'haddock' was Butler, which coincidently was also his profession. As soon as Butler entered the Blind Pirate Tavern, the murderous stares directed at him from the evil-hearted blaggards around the room increased his already nervous disposition tenfold. Slipping into his role quicker than he had the second-hand clothes he'd recently purchased from a drunkard—who seemed unfazed that his next drink, which he had hurriedly rushed off to seek out, would be purchased in his grubby underpants—Butler scowled, and with a brisk swipe of his hand, slammed the door shut. His next act of toughness was to spit on the floor, which he realized at that moment was something he should have practiced beforehand. Ignoring the dribble of spit running down the side of his shoe, he strolled as casually as he could to the bar. During a journey that seemed a lot longer than it actually was, he ignored the piles of vomit and bloodstains decorating the rough floorboards, the corpse in the corner with a gash in its throat deep enough to reveal the man's backbone, and the vicious stares of the rough-looking clientele. He was somewhat relieved when he finally reached his destination. He leant an arm on the sticky bar top, formed what he thought was a menacing don't-mess-with-me posture and looked at the bartender, who not surprisingly looked straight back at him.

"Beer!" Butler said in the toughest voice he could muster, which for someone of his upbringing and present nervousness, was a fair attempt.

The barman, not even mildly impressed, shook his head sadly and turned away to fulfil his customer's order.

Behind him, Butler heard the conversations in the room resume. His keen hearing picked out snatches of gossip far from normal and included topics he would rather have remained oblivious of.

Butler jumped when the barman slammed the beer, more dirty-brown foamy sludge than anything in liquid form, on the bar. Butler's expression was not one that displayed an eagerness to drink the frothy brew contained in the glass, well at least that's what he assumed the vessel was; it was so encrusted with grime it was difficult to recognize its true nature.

Butler's unfortunate display of obvious dissatisfaction at what had been served up was not lost on the keen-eyed barman, who quickly formed a similar expression of his own. From nowhere, a knife appeared in his hand. A blur of a hairy tattooed arm later, its point was buried in the bar top. "Summink wrong?"

Butler, already convinced by the barman's murderous tone that voicing a complaint would be an unwise, thought the quivering bloodstained knife a hair's breadth from his hand was unnecessary overkill. He glanced at the corpse in the corner, the two rats chewing on its carcass, then back at the disgruntled barman and smiled. "Something wrong? Of course not! I was just contemplating the delicious savouring of the fine beverage you have presented me, my good man."

The barman's puzzled expression informed Butler of two things: first, the barman was uneducated and failed to comprehend words of more than one or two syllables, and second, and perhaps of more importance to his current predicament, he had slipped from his role of ruffian and stood out like a giggling joke cracking clown at a funeral. He also became acutely aware of the hush that had again settled in the room and sensed every eye present was staring at him, except for the corpse's, though it did have a gaze that seemed to have followed his movements earlier. As far as he could see, and he was only looking as far as the door at this moment, he had two choices. He could either punch the rough, scar-faced, burly barman, grab the knife and with the weapon held menacingly—something he wasn't certain he could achieve—rush for the exit, or bluff his way out of the situation.

Butler decided on the latter. If that failed, he would grab the knife and run for the door like his life depended on him reaching it, as it undoubtedly would.

His false laugh convinced no one in the room. "I is only joking with yer, yer ugly son of a fat hideous sow," he told the barman, an individual whose smile he suspected was rarer than a clean glass in his establishment. Committed to his course, Butler ignored the barman's murderous scowl and continued. "I did rob a man 'bout a week ago and that was 'ow he spoke, all posh like. Made me wanna stick him, it did." He mimicked a stabbing with his hand, accidently knocking his unhygienic glass of dirty froth across the counter.

Surprisingly, the barman appeared to believe the story. He shrugged and slid the glass back to his customer. "Drink!"

Butler dragged his gaze from the man of little words and fewer syllables, and directed them at the foul drink he was not inclined to pour into his body.

The barman leaned a little closer. "If there be nothink wrong wit me beer, drink it!"

Suspecting no blood was going to be spilt in the next couple of minutes, the conversation in the room returned to its gruesome talk of thievery, murder and everything in-between.

With the sensation of being tied to a horseless carriage hurtling down a steep hill toward a cliff with a very steep drop, Butler reached for the glass, clasped reluctant fingers around its grimy surface, and trying to show no hesitancy, moved it toward lips that silently screamed in protest. Though he attempted to prevent the germ-ridden glass from touching his quivering lips and tip the foul brew directly into his mouth, the barman foiled his plan when he grabbed the bottom of the tankard and tipped. With a reluctance he had never experienced previously or ever wished to again, Butler let the disgusting brew claw its way down his throat.

Only when it was empty did the barman release his hold and stare at his customer expectantly.

Butler now realized the significance of the vomit littering the floor, and though he wished nothing more at that moment than to add a fresh patch, he knew to reveal his true reaction would probably end with his murdered body becoming company for the lone corpse in the corner. He forced his lips into a smile—more of a disgusted grimace really—and slammed the empty glass on the bar. Controlling the strong desire to gag, he wiped the dirty froth from around his mouth with the back of his hand and said as enthusiastically as he could, "Well, that was certainly summink. I don't think I 'ave ever tasted its like."

A smile that had more in common with a sneer struggled to form on the barman's grim features. "Yep, yer not be the first to say that," he said, proudly, reaching for the empty glass. "Yer want another?"

Frantically, Butler struggled to think up a refusal that would neither offend the man nor bring about his own demise. Just when he thought it wasn't possible, an excuse flashed into his thoughts. So pleased was he with the idea he inadvertently voiced his pleasure, "Brilliant!"

The Barman's look was a quizzical one. "Was that a yes?"

"Um, no. Though it would be *brilliant* to have another, I find myself low on funds, so unless the next is free..." Butler prayed it wasn't.

In a blur of movement, the dirty glass disappeared under the bar ready for the next unfortunate customer to be served a revolting beer from an equally revolting vessel. The barman rested one hand on the knife and stabbed the other at Butler. "Yer better ave a penny to pay fer that fine ale yer just supped or things are gonner get a might ugly fer yer, real quick like."

Though Butler could have presented a strong case about the man's ale being anything but fine, he kept quiet, fished a penny from his pocket and dropped it in a hand even grubbier than the tankard he had just drunk from, something that until that moment he believed to be an impossibility.

The barman glanced at the penny before slipping it into a pocket. "This ain't no charity house, so if yer skint, yer'd best be on yer way."

Though he had failed in his mission, Butler was rather eager to leave. Unfortunately, the hand that grabbed his shoulder decreed otherwise.

"It's alright, Scabs, his with me."

For some strange reason the barman slapped a hand over his nose, turned away and with a nervous hand gestured frantically for them to move away. It was obvious the barman was frightened of something, and as Butler knew it wasn't him, it had to be the person gripping his shoulder. He found himself spun around. His first impression of the not particularly tall man dressed in clothes that failed to complement each other so drastically they could only have been chosen for that sole purpose, was not of fear, but puzzlement. From the lopsided slightly crushed top hat to the eye-offending trousers, the man was the image of a jovial tramp. Though the man's eyes remained shadowed by the wide brim, the amount of face Butler could see framed by greasy brown hair was absent scars, somewhat of a rarity when compared to the tavern's present skin-disfigured clientele.

"Over here," said the fashion-challenged tramp when he turned and walked away.

Twitching his nose from a sudden bad smell, Butler checked the soles of his shoes. Both were free of the foul excrement he suspected may have been present. When he gazed after the strange fellow heading for the table positioned in the far corner of the room, he noticed those in his path leaned away from him and only returned to their former position when he had passed them by. To Butler, it seemed the man was feared by all in the room. The man's lack of scars could be an indication he was a skilled fighter able to dish out punishment without recciving any in return. He could be just the sort of man he needed, but if not, he might be acquainted with the type of specialist Butler required and the reason for his presence in this rough area of London where thieves and murderers had made their home.

Butler shot a glance at the door, and though he wished nothing more than to head through it, he instead walked over to the table where the man sat waiting for him. His stomach gurgled. He sighed; he feared he hadn't seen the last of the foul brew and the thought of it passing through his mouth once again was a nightmare he could never have envisaged before. He would ensure his master paid him a bonus for this, even if the miser wasn't aware he had.

Furtive watched the man he had been studying since he had first entered approach and the table sit opposite. He had soon arrived at the conclusion the man was an imposter and not a ruffian like the rest of the rabble currently occupying the room; this man had breeding. Intrigued to discover the man's purpose to risk his life in such a dangerous place, he asked, "So...what brings a man like yer to a rough place like this?"

Butler felt the urge to recheck his shoes for something he might have stepped in, but resisted. "I be looking fer a certain type."

Unseen by the man across the table, Furtive's shadow-concealed eyebrows rose. "What sort of type might yer be seeking? And yer can drop the phony talk. I knows yer ain't one of us."

Butler was relieved to do so. Words spoken in such a correct grammar deficient manner felt dirty on his lips. "I am looking for a type that I thought might be you."

"What—handsome, intelligent and well dressed?"

Butler already knew the man fell short of two of the descriptions and wasn't certain the other wouldn't soon join them. "No, I need someone who knows their way around other people's houses, if you know what I mean?"

Furtive knew exactly what he meant. "So, this type yer looking fer ain't exactly the law-abiding citizen type?"

Butler shook his head. "I would have no use for him if he was."

"It be a type with certain skills ter do a job yer ave in mind."

Butler nodded.

"What sort of job?"

Butler leaned forward. Sharp intakes of gasp-like breaths from those in the room caused him to turn to discover everyone in the inn staring at them.

"Ignore them," ordered Furtive. "They ain't got nothink better ter do than gawp."

Butler returned his gaze to the strange man and whispered, "I need some thieving done."

"Thieving, eh. What sort of thieving?"

Butler's nose twitched again. "I think you might have trod in something, I keep getting a whiff of something foul and unholy."

"My boots are clean," said Furtive, without looking. "I repeat: what kind of thieving?"

Butler leaned closer, something he would soon regret. "Burglary!"

"Okay, so...if I was of a type proficient in that skill, what would be me cut?"

A stench wafted over Butler, cloying his mouth with something so rank and disgusting he would risk another disgusting beer to rinse its foulness away. He now realized the reason for the others unwillingness to get close to this man. He sat back in his chair as far as he could, turned his head slightly to the side, and covered his nose with his hands.

Everyone in the room, except Furtive and Butler, roared with laughter.

Furtive sighed. "Okay, so I ave a bit of a problem in the fresh breath department..."

"A bit of a problem! I tell you right now I'd consider chewing a dog turd if it would rinse away the squalor currently dwelling in my mouth."

"Yes, I've heard it all before, now let's move on. If it be house thieving or any other kind, I'm yer man, but I need to know what I'll get out of it. As the barman so rightly stated, this ain't no charity house."

"One hundred pounds, cash," was Butler's muffled reply.

Furtive pondered the offer. *A hundred pounds was a lot of cash and something he desperately needed.* "Okay, I'll do it! When, where, what and who from?"

Butler informed Furtive of the job and a little about the miserly Ebenezer Drooge—how he had been in his service for nigh on twenty years, treated little better than a slave, received a pittance of a wage in return and that he had also tried to break into the safe himself, but had failed, which is why he needed the services of a skilled burglar.

When Furtive asked him why he had put up with Drooge and his rotten job for so long and not walked away, Butler told him the reason. Somewhere on the large estate was a fortune hidden by Ebenezer's grandfather, Jacobus Drooge. The family had searched for decades without success. He had only stayed for so long because he had also been looking for it.

Before Butler fled the Blind Pirate Tavern, never to return, Furtive insisted on an advance of ten pounds for expenses before he agreed to take on the job. To escape the man's breath, Butler would have willingly given him the whole hundred.

Two weeks later...

As Butler approached the study, he slapped his feet loudly on the tiled floor and paused outside with his ear against the door. From within the room came the chinking of glass, hurried slipper-clad footsteps crossing the room and lastly the creak of wicker. When all was silent, he opened the door. Framed in the doorway of the candlelit room, he glanced at the man feigning sleep in the wicker wheelchair. Butler shook his head in dismay, closed the door and coughed.

Ebenezer Drooge stirred with a convincing performance and sleepily opened his eyes. His fake yawn was accompanied by the exaggerated stretching of thin bony arms. His shrewd eyes glanced at Butler. "Is it time?"

Butler nodded. "Yes, Sir. If he has followed my instructions he will be waiting in the garden for this room to go dark."

"Let's hope this one succeeds where all those before have failed, or I'll likely be dead before I get my hands on it." Ebenezer's gaze strayed to settle on the brandy decanter across the room.

Butler picked up on the unspoken request and headed toward it. "Yes, Sir, so far results have been rather disappointing, but I have a feeling Furtive Freddy might surprise you."

"By surprise, I hope you don't mean he's going to jump out of the shadows with a loud yell. I'm not sure my poor heart could stand it."

"No, Sir, I am sure that is not on the burglar's agenda." Butler halted at the small table and stared at the level of brandy in the decanter, which was, in his estimation, two shots lower than when he had last laid eyes upon it. Beside the decanter a cut-crystal tumbler seeped fresh brandy fumes. "I think we may have a problem, Sir."

A worried frown appeared on the old man's wrinkled brow. "A problem! Explain yourself, man!"

Butler turned to look seriously at his employer. "I think Furtive may already be inside the house and has stolen some of your fine brandy, Sir, because it's lower than I remember."

Ebenezer's expression of anxiousness was replaced by guilty embarrassment. "Nonsense! It probably evaporated."

Butler raised his eyebrows. "I doubt that, Sir, as the top remains firmly seated." To prove the point, he lifted the decanter by its stopper.

"It must have been a mouse then."

Butler's eyebrows raised another notch. "A mouse, Sir? Then I suggest we contact the British Zoological Society to inform them of this event. Because if it were a mouse, as you have suggested, then it was clever enough to remove the stopper and strong enough to lift the decanter, pour brandy into a glass, replace the stopper and guzzle down the fine beverage without spilling a single drop. It would have to be a super strong and highly intelligent rodent to perform such a feat. Why, it could be a new super breed." He made to head toward the door, "Shall I rush off and send a telegram now, Sir?"

"Okay, okay, you've had your fun, Butler. I can see how impossible it would be for a mouse to have supped my brandy. It must have been the gardener."

Butler raised his eyebrows. "The gardener, Sir? Do you mean, one-armed Willy with the speech impediment?"

"That's the fellow. He always looked at me strangely with his shifty, cunning eyes."

"He was blind, Sir. His eyes couldn't be shifty or cunning if you popped them out and stuck them on a fox."

Ebenezer looked at Butler. "Are you telling me my gardener was blind, only had one arm and stuttered?"

Butler nodded. "He also had a dodgy hip and arthritis."

"Damn you man, who hired him?"

"That would be you, Sir. Apparently, he was extremely cheap."

"Then it's your fault, because I have to look after the pennies to pay your exorbitant wages."

"Exorbitant is not a label that could ever be attached to the pittance you pay me, Sir."

"Money is as money does, Butler."

Butler's puzzled expression revealed his failed attempt to make sense of the words.

Ebenezer glanced out the window at the moonlit garden below. "However, that explains the atrocious state of the garden. Sack the man, Butler. Can't have the staff pilfering my prized brandy."

"I would, Sir, but he died five years ago. So, unless his corpse rose from its grave and somehow managed to blindly stumble on malformed hips from the graveyard situated miles away, here to your manor, enter the house unheard and unseen and pour itself a brandy without spilling a drop, and then disappear without a trace, I am afraid we will have to discount that theory."

Ebenezer dismissed the matter with a weak wave of a frail limb. "I suppose we'll have to leave it as a mystery impossible to solve."

"Yes, Sir, I suppose we will." With a satisfied smirk, Butler poured brandy into the glass and carried it over to his master on a small silver tray.

The old man greedily took the offered beverage. "Ahh, just what the doctor ordered."

"Well, not really, Sir. He actually said, 'If you carried on drinking your liver would most probably commit suicide to escape the continued torment '"

"Bah! Doctors—they think they know everything."

"Yes, of course, Sir. It's not like they have to go through many years of extensive training before they can even assume the title of doctor."

"Exactly!" replied the old man, completely missing his manservant's sarcasm. He drained the glass in one and handed it to Butler.

"Now, Sir, I suggest we prepare to receive our visitor."

Ebenezer's eyes longingly followed the empty glass and watched it set down beside the tempting decanter.

"Shall I extinguish the candles, Sir?"

"Yes, and though I don't hold out much hope for success, I suppose we have to keep trying."

"If you want to find your grandfather's hidden inheritance, it is the only way, Sir. As I mentioned previously, I think Furtive might surprise us both." Butler snuffed out the candles and sat in a nearby chair.

A few moments later, concealed by the darkness in the room, wicker creaked, soft footsteps padded across the room, a clink of glass, splash of poured liquid, a satisfied gulp, soft footsteps and finally the creak of wicker.

Butler silently sighed.

Furtive noticed the room fade into darkness and smiled. It was time for him to do what he did best. He approached the house and made his way round to the back as Butler had instructed.

Like the windows adorning the front of the manor, those at the back were also barred. Furtive gazed up at the high roof. The small round skylight would be his point of entry, but first he had to reach it. There were two obvious options: the cast iron drainpipe, or the ivy that spread up to the gutter. He dismissed them both. Only amateurs would risk such obvious routes. Butler had warned him the house was well protected and to expect a few surprises.

His gaze settled on the branches of the ancient oak stretching out toward the roof. Though ending six feet short, he was confident he could make the jump.

He approached the tree and climbed it as proficiently as any squirrel. Once he had clambered up onto the first thick limb, the rest of the going was even easier. He climbed onto the highest branch strong enough to support his weight and ran along its length. On reaching its tip he launched himself into the air and sailed toward the house. His fingers gripped the gutter, his feet slammed silently against the wall. He climbed onto the lower roof, ran up the slates and paused on the ridge to survey his surroundings.

The round skylight set in the tower roof lay a short distance above. The warped and partly rotted wooden clapboards covering the side of the tower provided enough hand and foot holds to reach the gutter and pull himself up. A few careful strides up the steep slate roof brought him to the window. His experienced burglar eyes detected no sign of protection, only a simple metal catch locked the window. His knife slid between window and frame and slid the catch aside. He lifted the window that was hinged on its top edge and rested it against the sloping roof. He slithered inside and hung upside down with his feet hooked either side of the opening. The square of moonlight not blocked by his form, revealed little of the room or its contents. It did though reveal the tattered armchair directly below him; a soft landing only an amateur burglar would take advantage of.

He retrieved a small oil lamp fixed to a hoop from his pocket, lit it using the built-in auto-flint mechanism and slipped it over his hat anchored in place by its chin strap. Though most of the attic remained cloaked in darkness, the dim light illuminated his immediate surroundings. The wooden roof trusses stretched across the top of the room would provide a safe route to the door. Freeing one foot, he swung toward the nearest beam, grabbed hold and let his body drop. Using the momentum of his fall, he swung in a circle to land sure-footedly on top of the truss. He had made no sound. The only sign of his presence was the disturbed dust that drifted toward the jumble of unwanted objects littering the room. Five silent bounds carried him across the room. He dropped to land in front of the exit. His eyes studied the door, the frame and the large metal lock. When a turn of the handle failed to open the door, he knelt to examine the rusty lock more closely and smiled. It was a simple Walpole two-tumbler job. He could pick it in his sleep. He fished the required tool from a pocket, and in a blink of an eye and with a slight metallic scrape, the door was unlocked. He turned his attention to the hinges. They were rustier than the lock and would no doubt yell in protest when put to use. A drop of oil, a short wait and the problem was solved. Furtive turned the handle and pushed the door. It swung open without a sound.

Steps led down to another similar locked door, which was opened as expertly as the previous one. Furtive glanced furtively both ways along the door-lined corridor with a strip of worn carpet running down the middle. Except for the distant echoing sound of a ticking clock and creaks and groans of the old manor settling down for the night, silence reigned throughout the house. According to Butler's instructions, he needed to make his way to the library; there he would find Ebenezer's safe crammed with cash. He cautiously stepped into the hall and stared along its length. His finely attuned senses screamed a warning.

He dropped to his knees and lay on the floor. He removed the lamp from his head and held it at arm's length. The light revealed suspicious lumps in the carpet and thin, almost invisible trip wires stretched taut from wall to wall at various heights. He knew each would be attached to a bell or some other warning device to alert of an intruder's presence. His smile was one of admiration for the trap's conceiver.

Furtive slithered around to face in the opposite direction. He noticed two carpet lumps and two tripwires. He spent a moment planning his next course of action. Once decided upon, he replaced the lamp his hat, removed the Chinese vase from the nearby small table, set it softly on the floor and climbed on top. He leapt, grabbed the picture rail with strong fingers and sidled along in a direction that took him away from the grand staircase. Once past the cunningly designed traps, he dropped softly to the floor and before a door he believed would lead to an alternative route to the lower floor. A turn of the handle revealed it was unlocked. Cautiously, he pushed it open and smiled at the narrow staircase leading down. Furtive had robbed so many similar manors it was possible for him to discern the layouts of each, as most were built to a similar design. The staircase before him would have been used by the servants to move between floors without using the main staircase.

A quick survey of the stairs and walls convinced him they were trap free. Placing his feet at the far left and right sides of the treads, where they were less likely to creak, he gently lowered his weight onto each step during his descent. The door at the bottom, also unlocked, was soon passed through. He stood in a whitewashed corridor with doors opening onto the kitchen, scullery, stores, pantry and washroom, the working hub of the household where servants carried out the needs of their master. The appetizing aroma of cooking drifted from the kitchen and caused his empty stomach to rumble. Though he was tempted to go and have a quick taste, with an extreme effort he pushed the temptation aside and concentrated on the job in hand.

According to Butler, he was the only servant left. The old man, Drooge, could hardly walk and practically lived in a wheelchair, so he had no fear of the unexpected appearance of any household staff. Traps aside, it would be one of the easiest jobs he had ever done.

When he was satisfied the black and white tiled floor held no obvious danger, he made his way to the door at the end, which stood ajar. He peered through the gap. On his right he spied the bottom of the grand staircase and around the large tiled hall doors opened onto various rooms, but only one held any interest to him, the library. He scurried silently across the hall to the door indicated by Butler, who had assured him it would be unlocked. He reached for the handle. His fingers clasped around it. He paused. His senses were acting up again. He swivelled his head around the hall.

Ebenezer was growing bored and more than a little thirsty. "Do you think he's in the house yet?" he whispered.

"I am certain he is, Sir," replied Butler, softly.

"I haven't heard any traps sprung yet?"

"No, Sir. Then it's probably an indication he hasn't set any off. I told you I thought he might be the one."

The old man sniggered. "He's going to get a bit of a shock when he opens that safe and finds the surprise I left for him."

"Yes, Sir, I expect he will."

Ebenezer sniffed the air. "Oh, my god! What's that rank stench? Butler, you'll have to check my wheels when the lights are back on. You must have rolled in something foul when you last took me for a walk."

Darkness hid the surprised look on Butler's face. "No, Sir, I am afraid it's something much worse and not so easily wiped away."

The flare of the match Butler struck, lit up the darkness and glinted off the glass of brandy Furtive held in his hand.

Furtive raised the glass to the two men. "Cheers!" He swallowed it in one gulp and let out a satisfied smack of his lips. "That is by far the best brandy I have ever had the pleasure to drink."

"Butler, that man's stealing my brandy! It wasn't the mouse or the gardener's corpse, it was a him!"

Butler lit the candles. "Sir, I introduce to you, Furtive Freddy, a burglar of high caliber if his accomplishment this night is the evidence to consider."

"The only evidence I can see is the theft of my expensive brandy."

"I think he deserves a drink for his achievements this night, Sir," Butler argued. "He has made it through the house without setting off any traps, entered this room and poured himself a drink without alerting us to his presence."

Ebenezer shot a look at his brandy. "And I don't, I suppose?"

Butler fetched a clean glass from the cabinet, filled it with a double shot of brandy and took it over to Ebenezer, who snatched it from his grasp.

"Have you eaten, Furtive?" Butler enquired.

"Not since last Tuesday."

"Then would you like to join us for dinner in the adjoining room? There we can discuss what has happened this night."

"I must admit I am a little peckish." His stomach growled in agreement. "I am also curious as ter the reason fer the appalling deceit laid against me this night."

"Of course, Furtive, I promise all will soon be explained." Butler grabbed the handles of the wheelchair and pushed the old man toward the door. "Please follow me, Furtive."

"Will me 'undred quid also be served ter me as well as the grub?"

"Yes, Furtive, you will receive your fee minus the ten pounds you have already had."

The old man wrinkled his nose and grimaced. He leant over the side of the chair to look at the wheels. "You sure you haven't rolled me in some disgusting filth, Butler."

"Yes, Sir, I am absolutely certain."

2nd
CHAPTER

THE PLAN

On **entering the** dining room, Ebenezer cast a critical eye at the roaring log fire. "Rather excessive isn't it, Butler. Wood doesn't grow on trees you know."

"As we had a special guest, Sir, I thought you would want to make him comfortable. It is a rather cold house."

Ebenezer mumbled his displeasure. "Maybe you're right, but no more logs. The room's as hot as an oven."

"I could always assist you in removing some of your many layers of clothing, Sir, or those four woollen blankets you have cocooned yourself in."

The old man dismissed the thought with a wave of his hand. "Just serve the dinner. I'm famished."

"Of course, Sir." Butler wheeled his master to one end of the table where a place setting had been laid out and bade Furtive, whose eyes were busy casting an appreciative eye over the silver cutlery and serving platters, to sit at the opposite end.

"No, no! Butler, that won't do," moaned Ebenezer. "He's so far away I can barely see the man. We'd have to shout to hear one another. Seat him next to me."

"But, Sir, you don't..."

"No buts, just do as you're told, or you're fired."

"Again, Sir? We are nearing four figures now."

Ebenezer glared at him.

"Furtive, please move nearer to Mr. Drooge and I'll reset your place... No! On second thoughts, let me set your place before you move."

Furtive shrugged. "I'm easy any way yer want ter do it."

Butler quickly laid a place setting beside his master and withdrew to a safe distance. "All ready for you now, Furtive."

While Furtive moved along the long table, Butler disappeared to fetch the food he had prepared earlier. After a few trips, lamb stew, potatoes and vegetables were placed on the table. Standing at the opposite side of the table to Furtive, Butler dished out the food onto plates, placed one in front of Ebenezer and slid the other across the table to Furtive.

Furtive placed his face in the steam rising from the hot meal. "I believe that be the finest smell I have ever drawn up me nostrils. You cook it, did yer, Butler?"

Butler nodded. "Yes, Ebenezer sacked the cook, along with the rest of the staff, many years ago."

Ebenezer snorted. "Too damn right I did. It was a waste of money. Why employ five people to do a job one can do just as well?"

Furtive smiled. "That's very shrewd. One wage instead of five, even I know that makes good sense." He noticed no place setting set for Butler. "Yer not eating, Butler?"

"I eat in the kitchen. Staff do not eat with their employer."

"Bah! I told him there's no need for all this namby-pamby butler school etiquette and he's welcome to eat with me, but he won't hear of it." Ebenezer twitched his nose and then leaned forward to sniff his dinner. "Are you sure this meat is okay, Butler? It smells a bit rank."

"If the meat was any fresher, Sir, it would be running around the table, bleating."

"Bah! It must be your seasoning then."

"If you say so, Sir."

Furtive stuffed his mouth with a large forkful, chewed and swallowed. "Well, it tastes mighty delicious to me. Probably the best food I've ever had the pleasure ter stuff in me gob. Yer be a right good cook, Butler."

Butler gave Furtive a slight nod of thanks and turned to face his employer. "If you are confused by what Furtive so eloquently stated, Sir, it was a compliment."

"Bah" No profit in going around complimenting everyone. It's your job. You should be good at it."

"Not really it isn't, Sir, it was the cook's. I'm a butler, I '*butler*'."

Bored with the conversation, Ebenezer turned to Furtive. "So, Furtive, how long have you been in the burglary profession?"

Furtive paused with the heavily laden fork halfway to his mouth while he contemplated the question. "About thirty years now I suppose. I started when I was about six."

"Six!" exclaimed an astonished Ebenezer.

"Yeah, I know, I started late, but it was a family business and there were a lot of us, so I had to wait fer an opening. It came along when me cousin got caught robbing a magistrate's house. Unfortunately for me cousin, but obviously lucky for me, he stood before the same magistrate he tried ter rob. Got a hanging sentence he did." Furtive stuffed so much food into his mouth it bulged his cheeks.

"You come from a long line of burglars, then?" Butler asked.

Food sprayed from Furtive's mouth when he answered. "Sure do, me pappy, his pappy, and his pappy's pappy and so on till I don't know when. My great-grand pappy often joked there was one of our line hanging on the cross next to Jesus, we go that far back."

"An impressive pedigree," stated Ebenezer, watching his guest grab a potato in a grubby claw and cram the whole thing in his mouth.

With crushed potato oozing from his lips, Furtive pointed his fork at Ebenezer. "Yer wanna know a secret?" Though a tongue of an indescribable colour flicked out to scoop up dribbles of fleeing potato, it failed to catch the trickle of gravy oozing down the burglar's chin.

Ebenezer, too appalled by the man's table manners to speak, nodded his assent and leaned closer to the man.

"I wouldn't do that..."

Butler's warning was hushed by a frantic wave of his employer's frail hand; Ebenezer was not the sort to be able to resist the unveiling of a secret.

Butler grinned when Furtive leaned nearer to Ebenezer. Fun was in such short supply nowadays.

"It concerns my great uncle, Percy Pickles..."

Ebenezer's features formed a strange, mystified expression. His face flushed green as he gagged. With his curiosity to learn the secret totally forgotten, he shot back with such force the creaking chair shot back a foot. His expression was of someone who had just faced hell and wasn't sure they were going to survive the experience. His glazed, horrified expression turned to look at his guest in abject horror.

Furtive, apparently unaware or unconcerned by what had just happened, paused telling to shove more food into his mouth.

"My god man, what vile hell-spawned breath you have. It's fouler than your table manners, something I thought impossible a moment ago. I am sorely tempted to cut off my nose so I can never smell its foulness again."

Furtive shrugged. "What can I say, there's nothink I can do about it."

"Nothing you can do! Have you tried cleaning your teeth?"

"Yeah, I tried it once, it didn't work."

"Once! You have to clean them twice every day."

Furtive snorted in disbelief. "Twice! Every day! Who does that?"

"Nearly everyone except you, I expect," said Butler, who relocated his master to the other side of the table. "Are you still eating, Sir?"

"No, I am damn well not. I doubt I'll ever eat again. My mouth feels like it's been used as a curry house toilet. I tell you Butler, if there was acid handy I'd rinse my mouth with it to be free of the putrid taste."

"I know, Sir, I have previously experienced Furtive's corpselike breath."

"And you didn't think to warn me?"

"I did try, Sir."

"Not very damn hard you didn't."

Furtive pushed his plate away. "I couldn't eat another thing. I'm fit to burst."

A look of horror appeared on Ebenezer's face. "God forbid such a thing will ever occur in my presence," he shivered with revulsion at the thought. "For your breath to stink like it does, your insides must be a long way past rotten."

"Okay, I get it. Me breath's not as fresh as it could be. Live with it and let's move on. I thought we had business to discuss?"

"I'm not sure I want to go into business with you now," said Ebenezer, adamantly.

Furtive jumped to his feet. "If that's the case, hand over me 'undred pounds and I'll be on me merry way."

"Let's not all be so hasty," said Butler, attempting to bring order to the room. "And it was ninety."

"Furtive, I am sure you can understand that your... affliction, is a bit of a shock when encountered, especially when the receiver has not been forewarned of its potency and so able to protect themselves against it as best they can."

Furtive resumed his seat. "Aye, I can understand that right enough."

Butler turned to his employer. "Sir, we have been searching for someone with Furtive's burglary talents for some time now, if you refuse to work with him, it would mean starting again. Something which, at your advanced age, I am sure you are loathe to do."

Ebenezer nodded his agreement. "What do you suggest?"

"I suggest we inform Furtive of the reason we have sought out a man of his talents and see if he is agreeable to our terms and would be willing to participate in our quest."

Ebenezer relented. "Okay, inform him of our needs."

Butler turned to Furtive. "As you may have already guessed, breaking into this house tonight was a test to discover if you were the right thief for the job."

"Yeah, I guessed that part easy enough."

"From what we have discussed you are also aware you passed the test and we want you to join us in a scheme where your talents will be in great demand."

"And what exactly is this plan of yours? Yer obviously want something pinched from somewhere and I'm guessing this somewhere ain't that easy ter get into."

"Correct, not easy at all. Ebenezer's grandfather amassed a large fortune and due to the miser streak running through the family line, he wasn't about to trust any bank with his hard-earned wealth. What he did instead was to hide it. Unfortunately, he was kicked in the head by a horse and died instantly, taking the location of his treasure to the grave with him."

"The only clues to its whereabouts," said Ebenezer, taking over the telling, "was in two paintings." His hand indicated a painting of average size hanging above the fireplace. "One like that; the other is in possession of someone else."

"Then it's a painting yer want me ter steal?"

Ebenezer nodded. "Exactly! Only when I am in possession of the two will I be able to work out the clues to the treasure's location."

"Who owns the other one?"

"That would be my brother, Sebastian Drooge."

"But if this treasure is so vast, why don't you and Sebastian work together ter find it and split it down the middle."

"Bah! Because he refuses to even entertain such a notion."

"The problem is, Sabastian is even more of a miser than Ebenezer, something which even I find hard to believe, but it's true," Butler explained. "They were never the best of friends, but now they have become sworn enemies. Getting one over on the other has become almost as important as finding the inheritance. Sebastian has tried to steal Ebenezer's painting many times and vice-versa, without success. Even if he does succeed, the painting you see hanging here is a copy with certain details left out and others added. The original is safely hidden to guard against theft."

"We suspect my brother has done the same as a precaution against me stealing his," added Ebenezer.

"I assume his original is also hidden in a secure place," enquired Furtive.

"It is," said Butler. "However, we believe we know the room it's hidden in is deep below the castle, but not where in that room it is, which is why we need someone of your talents to find it. We found this out when I tracked down a staff member Sebastian sacked when he suspected the man of stealing some silver," he pointed at Furtive, "similar I suppose to the knife and fork I suspect are concealed within a secret pocket of your coat."

Furtive unashamedly fished the food stained cutlery from the concealed pocket and placed them on the table. "I'm a thief, stealing is what I do."

"I assure you, if you agree to help us and are successful in that endeavour, there will be no need for you to ever turn to petty thievery again, because you will be a rich man."

Furtive looked at Ebenezer. "What, more than the 'undred pounds I'm already owed?"

"Ninety," Butler corrected.

Ebenezer nodded. "Much more. One hundred times more to be exact."

For a few moments Furtive's brain whirred to calculate the sum; it was painful to witness. "One thousand pounds!"

Butler started to correct the man's mistake. "No..."

Ebenezer held up a hand to silence Butler. "Don't interrupt when I'm talking business." With a miserly grin upon his lips, he turned to face the man whose mathematical proficiency was at the exact level he liked when negotiating terms. "Yes, Furtive, a whopping one thousand pounds."

"Wow! I don't rightly know what to say. I don't suppose there ain't much you can't buy with that amount of money."

Butler sighed.

"So, Furtive, you're in? You accept the job and the terms laid out before you?"

"If it includes the 'undred I've already been promised, then, yes, Ebenezer, I accept the job and the terms. I'd be a bloody fool not to, wouldn't I?"

Butler sighed.

Ebenezer rubbed his hands together in a satisfied greedy fashion only a miser can perfect. "I'd shake your hand to seal the deal, but however far I managed to stretch my old limb I would still be too close to that cesspit mouth of yours. I would rather be sealed in an airtight room with a dozen aggressive skunks than risk getting a whiff of that unholy stench again. No offense intended, of course."

"I assure you, Mr. Ebenezer, none is took."

"What we'll do is seal the bargain in a different, and I'm sure you'll agree, a much more pleasant fashion. Butler, fetch the brandy."

"Now yer be speaking me own language, Mr. Ebenezer, Sir."

Butler sighed forlornly and went to do his master's bidding.

3rd
CHAPTER

SEBASTIAN
DROOGE

"**Come in!**" **called** out Sebastian Drooge, a little brusquely.

A man as shabby as he was villainous entered a room adorned with books. Light from electric lanterns highlighted the spines of the thousands of volumes standing proudly upright like soldiers on parade in dark oak bookcases. The room smelled of polish and musty pages, but to Sebastian Drooge it was the fragrance of knowledge. Though he had not read every book on display, a vast amount of the dusty tomes had received the pleasure of his knowledge seeking attention.

Sebastian marked the page of the book he had been reading with a thin strip of blue silk ribbon attached to the spine and gently closed it. Only after he had climbed to his feet and placed the thick volume back in the vacant space in one of the bookshelves did he turn to address his visitor.

"Well?" he questioned.

"Yer were right, Sir, he is up to something. The man Butler met in London is a thief who goes by the name of Furtive Freddy. Apparently, he's a bit dim but very good at what he does. He arrived at yer brother's manor earlier tonight and entered through the roof. A short while later I saw him talking and having dinner with Ebenezer and Butler. Though I couldn't hear what was said, it looked like their talk was of the conspiring type."

"Yes, I'm sure it was." Sebastian turned to look at the twin painting to Ebenezer's hanging on the wall.

As Ebenezer surmised, it was also a copy with details not true to the original.

He turned back to face the man waiting patiently for attention. "Is the burglar still at Ebenezer's?"

"He was when I left to come and make my report to yer. I 'ave two men watching the house, front and back, so if he leaves we'll know about it."

Sebastian spent a few moments in thoughtful contemplation. "If they have formed a plan with this furtive thief, as I suspect they have, he will stay at the house until they come here and attempt to steal my painting. What they don't know is that I will be prepared for them." He walked around his desk and up to the man. "Do you have more men you can call into service?"

"I do. Tell me how many and what yer want them to do and I'll arrange it."

"Double the lookouts at the house and double the guards here, and contact Crakett Murdersin, tell him the time is near and he is to come here to finalize the arrangements."

"Yes, Sir. Will that be all?"

"Yes, Flint, that will be all. You have done well thus far. Continue to so and a bonus could be coming your way, fail me and it will be my dagger."

"Thank you, Sir, I understand and will not let you down." He left the room and closed the door softly.

Sebastian's eyes wandered back to the painting. A smirk broke his usual persistent frown. *Soon it would be in his grasp. When Ebenezer's men come to rob me, mine will be at his house robbing him.* He almost laughed, evilly.

LURCH

Ebenezer sipped his third deal celebration brandy as Furtive downed his third in one gulp and stared longingly at the decanter on the table. "Have another if you..."

Furtive had grabbed the decanter on *'have,'* filled his glass on *'another,'* drunk it on *'if'* and with empty glass clutched in grubby hands, stared longingly at the decanter on *'you.'*

"Now we have sealed our bargain, it is time to turn to other matters, the details of our plan. "A nod of Ebenezer's head and worried frown at the brandy, prompted Butler into movement.

Furtive's sad eyes followed the decanter being relocated far from his reach. Accepting no more brandy was coming his way any time soon, he reluctantly placed the glass on the table.

"However," Ebenezer continued, "As we will no doubt encounter confined spaces during the execution of the robbery, I think it's essential for the health of anyone coming into your proximity, we at least try to somehow lessen the effect of your rotten odorous breath."

"Shall I fetch the acid and a very stiff broom, Sir?"

"Not yet, Butler, I'm hoping it won't come to that. We'll try something less severe first. Furtive, however long and hard I search my intelligent brain, I can't think of a more stupid question than the one I am about to ask you, but here goes. Do you have a toothbrush?"

"Matter of fact, Mr. Ebenezer, Sir, I think I might." Furtive plunged a hand into a pocket, there was a clatter of whatever objects he had concealed within moving about and then his hand reappeared holding a toothbrush, which he displayed proudly to the astonished onlookers."

"You were right, Butler, he has surprised me."

"But... that's my toothbrush!" stated Butler, unhappily, staring at his black and white butler themed toothbrush.

"I found it when I had a wander around yer house after I opened the safe and realized I'd been duped. I tell yer Mr. Ebenezer, if yer 'ave any valuables yer certainly 'ave 'em well hidden."

Astonishment creased Ebenezer's wrinkled features. "You opened the safe! But how? We heard nothing."

"That's because I didn't go in through the front ter set off yer little surprise. I suspected something weren't quite right about all this, so I nipped into the secret passage between the walls and went in from the back."

Ebenezer's astonishment increased. "Secret passage! What secret passage?"

"The one accessed through the secret door in the wooden panelling in yer office of course."

Ebenezer was so amazed, he said so. "I'm amazed. I had no idea it was there."

"When yer've robbed as many big houses like this as what I 'ave, yer gets to smell 'em."

"If there were any doubts he wasn't the right man for the job, there can't be now, ay Butler." He looked at his servant and noticed the man's dismayed expression and the finger pointed at Furtive accusingly. "What's got into you, man? Lower that incriminating arm immediately?"

"But that's my special limited-edition butler toothbrush!"

Ebenezer shrugged. "I can't see the problem. You can have it back when he's finished with it. You'll just have to share until we can buy him a new one."

Butler shivered with revulsion and almost gagged at the thought of something entering his mouth after it had been in Furtive's. It was bad enough something of his was being held in the burglar's germ encrusted fingers; God knows what foul areas of the man's body they had previously probed. He sighed it loss.

"Furtive, I want you to take your toothbrush..."

"*My* toothbrush!"

Ebenezer ignored Butler. "...and go to the washroom beside the kitchen. There, you will give your teeth a good scrub and afterwards rinse your mouth a few times with lavender water you'll find..."

"...it's okay, I know where it is; I saw it earlier when I was having a nose about."

"Then directions to the washroom are also obsolete!"

Furtive grinned as he stood. "They most certainly are."

"By the time you return, the fourth member of our gang should be here for you to meet."

"Would that be the muscle?"

Ebenezer raised his unruly eyebrows. "How did you know?"

"Easy, you're the client, Butler's the brains and I'm the specialist. Only thing that's missing is the muscle."

"You are not half as stupid as the impression you give."

"Why thank you, Mr. Ebenezer." He headed for the door.

Ebenezer and Butler watched him leave.

"What do you think of him, Sir?"

"I think he is perfect for what we have planned, and he comes at a fraction of the price I expected to pay."

"Yes, about that, Sir. It's not really fair is it, you know, considering what he has to do."

"Life isn't fair, Butler. You of all people should know that; you work for me."

"Of course, Sir. How silly of me to forget."

"Anyway, if Furtive does as well as I believe he will, I'll give him a bonus."

Butler clutched his heart in mock pain. "Sir, I really wish you'd warn me when you are going to say something so out of character. I nearly had a heart attack."

"Very droll, Butler. You always paint me in a bad light, except for that one time," he smiled at the memory, "but it's not true."

"Once again, Sir, I must apologize. It must be something to do with knowing you for more years than I care to count and never, ever, hearing you mention the bonus word in such a context."

"Apology accepted. If a bonus is deserved, he shall have one; I'll let him keep your toothbrush."

"How extremely generous of you, Sir, to give away something you neither own nor want."

"I know, I think I'm mellowing as I get older. Now, pass me the speaking tube so I can tell Lurch to come down and meet the new addition to our team."

Butler walked to the wall, unhooked the end of a tube from a bracket and stretched it over to Ebenezer.

Ebenezer removed the cap and put it to his ear. "I can't hear him snoring so maybe for once he hasn't fallen asleep."

"I find that doubtful, Sir."

Ebenezer held the tube out. Butler leaned toward it and blew a shrill whistle into the pipe. Ebenezer returned it to his ear and giggled. "He just cursed. Now his moving about. Footsteps getting closer." He suddenly ripped the speaking tube from his ear and replaced it a few moments later. "How many times do I have to tell you, Lurch, YOU DON'T NEED TO SHOUT!... What do you mean you don't know?... What? Four or five? No, that's not the answer; the question was rhetorical... oh, never mind." He shook his head in dismay. "Just get down here. We are in the dining room."

Butler replaced the listening tube.

"If that man had one more brain cell it would still be lonely."

"Yes, Sir, but he means well. I suppose when Furtive returns we'll have to tell him about the disguise."

"Oh, goody, a disguise. What, like a wig and a moustache? I always fancied one of those big long ones." He mimicked stroking a long handlebar moustache. Not too keen on a beard though, made me all scratchy when I tried to grow one before, but if the job calls for it, I'll grin and bear it."

Ebenezer and Butler stared at Furtive sitting at the table with a glass of brandy in his hand. Their gazes flicked from the firmly closed door he would have had to pass through, to the decanter directly between them.

"How did you do that?" asked Butler.

Furtive shrugged. "I'm a burglar, I burgle!"

"But we didn't hear the door open, a clink of class, or anything. Not a sound!"

"I don't know why yer so surprised. I wouldn't be a very good burglar if I stomped around whistling, would I?"

Butler shook his head. "I suppose not."

Booming footsteps echoed throughout the house. The chandelier swung. The crystal lid of the decanter clinked. The loud footsteps approached the room and suddenly the door swung open with such force it slammed against the wall, causing a painting to crash to the floor.

Furtive cocked a finger toward the large man filling the doorway. "Now, he could never be a burglar."

Lurch guiltily bent his broad shoulders to peer around the doorframe at the broken picture and then looked at Ebenezer. "Sorry, Boss."

"I'll deduct it from your wages, now shut the door and come here."

Butler noticed the look of dilemma appear on Lurch's face. "Come in, shut the door gently and then come here, Lurch."

The big man did as requested, and stood near Furtive.

Butler introduced the two men. "Lurch, this is Furtive."

Furtive stuck out an arm. "Nice to meet yer, Lurch."

"That's not advisable if you want to retain the use of your hand," Butler warned quickly.

By the speed at which Furtive snatched his hand away it was obvious he did.

"Hello, Mr. Furtive. It is nice to meet you also."

Ebenezer looked at Furtive, paying particular attention to his mouth. "Did you give your teeth a good hard scrub and rinse?"

Furtive smiled in reply and dragged back his lips.

"Well, they do look slightly less grubby," observed Ebenezer from afar. "Lurch, lean down nearer Furtive."

Without hesitation, Lurch did as he had been ordered.

Furtive, please exhale a deep breath in his face."

"Sir," protested Butler. "Are you sure that's wise?"

Ebenezer glared at Butler. "Would you rather carry out the test? I'm sure Lurch won't mind."

Butler remained silent.

"Furtive, please continue."

Butler grimaced and turned his head slightly to one side.

Ebenezer smiled, held a corner of a blanket over his nose and watched to see what Lurch's reaction would be; he expected the worst.

Furtive breathed out a long huff of air strong enough to ruffle Lurch's rebellious sideburns.

Whereas Butler was surprised by Lurch's lack of reaction, Ebenezer was a little disappointed.

With his voice muffled by the blanket, Ebenezer issued his next instructions, "Lurch, bend closer. Furtive, repeat the process with a bit more oomph."

Though confused by the strange request, Lurch nevertheless did as ordered and positioned his face close to Furtive's.

Furtive huffed in the big man's face with such force Lurch's fringe stood to attention.

Again, Lurch showed no reaction. He turned his head and looked at his employer for further instruction.

Ebenezer cautiously removed the blanket. "Do you smell anything, Lurch?"

Lurch shook his head.

"Are you sure?"

Lurch nodded.

Ebenezer smiled. "I must admit I am more than a little surprised. You must have given them a really good clean, Furtive."

"That I did, Ebenezer, Sir, a right good scrub and a thorough rinse with that there lavender water."

"Lurch, you can stand up now," said Butler.

The creak of wicker accompanied Ebenezer's journey around to the other side of the table. He halted beside Furtive. "Breathe on me, just a little mind."

Furtive breathed.

Ebenezer's eyes rolled into the back of his head and his lips curled back in a grimace not thought possible by a human until that moment. His nose tried to wrench itself from its face and leap into the fire. His body, keen to put as much distance between itself and the offending fumes, slammed into the back of the wheelchair; the force sent it rolling across the room until it was halted by the wall.

Butler leapt into action, no, that was a lie; he grinned, almost snickered even, casually poured a shot of brandy into a glass and whistling a merry tune, strolled over to the comatose form of his employer. He waved the brandy under the man's nose, tipped a little into his gaping mouth and stood back.

Ebenezer shot upright and screamed loud enough to be heard in three counties. "Arrghhhhhh! Hands swiped at his lips. His nose twitched so violently everyone who saw it thought it would fly off. "Kill me, please someone kill me and bury me so deep the foulness that covers me can never seep out. My body feels like it has been violated by the foulest creatures ever to be spawned in the deepest, darkest depths of hell where even demons fear to tread. He spat, and he spat, and he spat in an effort to free himself of the putrid taste. He grabbed the brandy Butler held out, poured it into his mouth, swished, gurgled and spat it out. His hand shot out. "More, much more! He glared at Furtive. "What in hell's name just happened? Why wasn't Lurch affected?"

Furtive shrugged. "Maybe you have a sensitive nose."

"Not anymore I haven't. It's so fouled I don't think I'll be able to smell anything pleasant again." He took the replenished glass from Butler and with narrowed eyes turned his attention to Lurch. "You sure you didn't smell anything?"

"I smelt nothing, honest Boss." Then, as if he had remembered something, guilt swept over his face.

"Lurch! What is it Lurch! Tell me!"

"Sorry Boss, I forgot."

"What exactly did you forget?"

Lurch's fingers went to his nostrils and pulled out two balls of candle wax. "I was told it stops you from snoring. I know how you hate my snores, because they're so loud and thundering, so I thought I'd try it." He smiled. "I think it worked. That's good, ain't it Boss?"

Ebenezer fumed.

"Lurch!" said Butler. "Return to your post, now!"

Lurch quickly lurched across the room and slammed the door behind him. Another picture fell to the floor and smashed. "Sorry boss."

Without seeming to have moved from his seat, Furtive had a full glass of brandy and the decanter was empty.

Ebenezer tilted his head back and screamed.

Butler sighed and wished he'd chosen another profession.

5th CHAPTER

FURTIVE'S DISGUISE

Twenty minutes later, Butler entered the lounge to find the burglar waiting for his return. It was obvious by his relaxed position in one of the comfortable easy chairs and his feet resting on the antique coffee table, the man had made himself at home. If any additional evidence was needed, it was provided by the full glass of brandy held in one hand and the smouldering cigar in the other. Butler's gaze shot to the cabinet where the aforementioned luxuries were stored under lock and key. The small door showed no sign of damage. He fished a key ring from his pocket and searched among them, the cabinet key was present.

Furtive glanced over at Butler and shook his head. "I don't need keys. I'm a burglar."

Butler returned the keys to his pocket and approached the liberty-taking thief. "Yes, something that is very apparent, but while you are in this house there has to be rules, you can't..." His finger shot towards Furtive like a dagger. "You're wearing my dressing gown!"

"Oh, it's yours is it? I found it. Discarded it was. Just lying there, so I didn't think anyone would mind."

"You were wrong, someone does mind. Me!" Butler screwed up his eyes suspiciously. "By 'discarded' and 'just lying there,' do you mean it was in my bedroom hanging on a coat-hanger in my wardrobe?"

Furtive nodded. "Yeah, I suppose I do."

"This has to stop! You have to stop helping yourself to things that don't belong to you while you are in this house, but especially my personal things."

Furtive shook his head adamantly, dislodging an inch-long wad of ash from the cigar that rolled down the dressing gown. "Sorry, no can do. It's against the *Code*."

Butler snatched up an ash tray and placed it on the arm of the chair Furtive occupied like he was the lord of the manor. "What code?"

"The burglar's code of course: Pay fer nothing! Steal everything*!"*

"Yeah, well butler's have their own code: You touch anything what don't belong to you in this house again and Lurch will pull your arms off.*"*

Furtive snorted. "That ain't no code. Yer just made it up ter fit this 'ere situation. A code has got ter be catchy like. Short, but meaningful. *Pay fer nothing! Steal everything*! That's a real genuine code, that is."

"You'll find out just how meaningful my code is if you dare lay your grubby hands on my stuff again."

"Okay, okay, I get yer message, *don't touch yer stuff.*" He took another puff of the cigar, dislodging more ash.

"And use the damn ashtray!"

Furtive exaggeratedly flicked ash in the ashtray. "I'm using it. I'm using it. Jesus! Yer gotta learn ter relax a bit."

"I *was* relaxed until you set foot in the house."

"Plonk yerself down on the sofa. I poured yer a brandy."

Butler glanced at the glass on the coffee table, sat down on the sofa and took a sip.

"Look, I ain't promising nothink, but I'll try ter behave a bit better. Where's the old man?" Furtive asked. "Alright is he?"

"I'm not sure he will ever be alright again. He felt so soiled after you breathed on him he's taking a bath hot enough to make a scalding pot of tea."

Furtive smiled. "That were right funny though, weren't it?"

Butler grinned. "I must admit, it did bring me a certain amount of amusement."

They laughed.

"Is his bathroom at the top of the stairs, the one with the big enamel bath?"

Butler nodded.

Furtive smirked. "I thought it was. Now, Butler, tell me about this disguise I haf ter wear!"

"It's not just a disguise; you also have to impersonate someone."

"Look like me then. does this fella I'm ter impersonate?"

"I wouldn't say there is much of a resemblance, though you are both of a similar height, sort of."

"That's the reason for the disguise, ter make me look like him?"

Butler nodded.

"Must be a damn good disguise if yer think it'll make me look like someone who looks nothink like I do."

"Oh, believe me, it is. No expense has been spared."

"Whats this fella look like?"

Butler fished a hand into his pocket and pulled out a photograph. "Better I show you." He slid the photograph across the table.

Furtive picked it up and studied the sepia image. His eyebrows rose so high they nearly disappeared over the back of his head. "Oh man, that's some ugly creature. Yer sure it's even human? And what's it got on its back? And that hair, terrible. I've seen brooms with better style."

"Oh, he's human sure enough. That thing on his back is part of him; he's a hunchback."

Furtive stared at Butler doubtfully. "Yer have a disguise that'll turn someone as handsome and stylish as me into that?"

"Yes, with a few alterations I don't foresee a problem. You still want the job?"

Furtive dropped the photograph on the table. "If yer think it's important to the plan, then count me in. For a thousand pounds I'd dress up as the rear end of a donkey, cover meself in blood and walk into a lion's den shouting dinner's ready."

Butler smiled at the image that appeared. The man's foul breath would certainly help convince the lions it was the back end of a donkey calling out to them. "The disguise is perhaps the most essential part of the plan, because it will allow you to gain entry to Sebastian's castle with his blessing."

"I take it this hunchback is something special if Sebastian has hired him. Who is he?"

"His name is Craaketaaat Murrrrrderrrrsinnnn*!"*

A little surprised, Furtive stared at Butler. "Why'd yer say his name all spooky like?"

Butler shrugged. "Just setting the tone. By all accounts Crakett Murdersin has an evil personality. Have you heard of him?"

"Oh, I've heard of him. It's right what yer've heard, he's a nasty piece of work alright; mad, bad and dangerous to know. Definitely not a man yer want to meet if yer can avoid it. I heard he murders people just for fun if there's even a hint of an excuse ter do so. I was told a story about one of his evil deeds a while ago, if you want to hear it?"

Butler nodded he did.

"Crakett did a job for Four Fingers Finnigan; the vicious boss of a gang of murderous cutthroats, thieves and ne'er-do-wells, but when Finnigan welches on his end of the deal and refuses to pay him, Crakett breaks in ter his place the same night and steals from the man's stashed hoard of ill-gotten valuables ter the cost of his fee, plus a bit extra for the inconvenience, quite a bit extra I believe. Of course, Finnigan wasn't at all happy about this and plonks a reward on his head. Crakett hears about this and he also weren't happy. Bold as brass he strolls into Finnigan's lair, an old abandoned factory down by the docks, and straight to his face like, he tells Finnigan he either drops the reward or the only head ter be taken would be Finnigan's own and anyone else's who tries to stop him."

Furtive sat forward in his seat. "Yer haft to picture this, Butler, Crakett is in the man's home. Finnigan is sitting on his throne atop a pile of packing cases like the king of the manor, which he was, and Crakett is surrounded by Finnigan's gang of vicious cutthroats, who are armed to the teeth. And yer ain't gonna believe this, but the only weapon Crakett has was a *fruit-knife*. A damn tiddly little fruit-knife, and apparently, not all that sharp."

"Seems a rather strange choice of weapon under the circumstances," said Butler.

"He was making a point, yer see. The boss's men had knives, big un's mind, swords, clubs with nasty long spikes, pistols and blunderbusses. Crakett shouldn't have stood a chance in hell of surviving."

Butler, so engrossed in the story, almost leaned nearer to its orator, but remembering what an unwise move that would be, remained with his back firmly pressed against the sofa. "Did Finnigan do as Crakett asked and rescind the reward?"

Furtive snorted. "Like heck he did. Finnigan sees this hunchback armed with a tiny blade, which by the look of its dull edge wouldn't pierce the skin of an over ripe tomato, his men fully armed; some with more than one weapon, no way is he gonna back down. He tells Crakett exactly that and orders his men ter kill the intruder." Furtive paused to sip his drink and puff on the cigar.

Butler, keen to hear the outcome, bade Furtive to continue.

"What happened next still remains a bit of a mystery. Crakett is attacked by thirty men and when the clash of steel, gunshots and screams of mortal agony fall to silence, Finnigan stares at the cloud of dust raised by the fight. When it clears, the only two men alive in the room are him and Crakett."

Butler's well-trimmed eyebrows rose. "He killed them all!"

"He sure did, and all with his little fruit-knife. Anyway, Finnigan is shocked, anyone would be who had just witnessed such a devastating event. He stares at Crakett holding that tiny knife, now stained with the blood of his dead men, and Crakett standing there casually with his foot on the head of Finnigan's second in command. Beside him is a neat pyramid formed out of his thugs' heads, but it don't end in a point, there's two heads missing to complete the macabre construction. With a flick of his foot, Crakett flips the head onto the top of the pyramid. Now only one head is needed ter complete the gruesome sculpture and Finnigan is well aware whose head Crakett wants to use. If Finnigan weren't happy before, he's damn livid now. His gang of murderous cutthroats took a long time to assemble. He knows he can't just go and pick such fine men off the street. So, as to be expected, he rises from his throne— a mouldy old armchair with a grandiose name— pulls out a pistol with one hand and a pirate sword believed to have once belonged to Blackbeard, with the other, and slowly like, he climbs down the steps towards the man responsible for slaying his men..." Furtive unexpectedly stopped.

"Go on, don't stop now. What happened next?" urged Butler.

"Sorry, I told yer there was a mystery attached, that be all I know. I was in an inn at the time listening to the story, but had to scarper when someone, a vicious sort mind yer, make no mistake about that, who had a grudge against yours truly, entered. As soon as he laid eyes on me he drew a knife, a lot, lot, bigger than Crakett's fruit cutting utensil. In fact, it was so big the long shadow it cast enabled me to creep away and out the door unseen. The result is I never did hear the end of that tale."

Butler was more than a little dismayed. "The only mystery I can see is why you would start a story you don't know the finish of?"

Furtive shrugged. "Even lacking an ending it's still a great story. Crakett obviously survived, equally obvious is that he killed the boss, cut off his head and stuck it on top of the ghastly pyramid."

"No! You can't assume that. Maybe the boss escaped, or they came to some sort of arrangement?"

"Unlikely, from what I've heard..."

"...Which again, probably isn't the full story."

Furtive ignored the interruption. "From what I've heard, Crakett Murdersin ain't the arrangement making type when it comes ter anyone he has a grievance against."

The two men sat in silence for a few moments.

Butler broke the lull in conversation. "Even though you are aware of how dangerous Crakett is, and his unforgiving revengeful nature, you have no concerns about impersonating him?"

"I wouldn't say I am concern free, but I assume yer have a plan ter handle the situation, because if I am in danger then so is yerself and the old man."

"The plan I have devised, though not risk free, is rather a good one," Butler stated proudly.

Furtive grinned. "Cunning plan, is it?"

"So cunning you could stick a tail on it and call it a weasel. Do you want to hear it?"

"It's probably important to a successful outcome that I do."

"Sebastian has been in contact with Crakett Murdersin, who's currently lodged in The Beggar's Arms hotel in Whitechapel. I have a man watching him and have bribed the inn-keeper to intercept all correspondence he receives. What we have learnt so far is that Sebastian plans to steal Ebenezer's painting in five days, on the night of the Christmas Eve annual ball, which is held a couple of miles away at Havasham Manor. Both Sebastian and Ebenezer will be attending; it's a traditional event they both never miss. Sebastian also suspects we will attempt to steal his painting on the very same night, which we will. Even at this very moment he has men watching Drooge Manor. They also followed you here, something we were aware of and used to our advantage.

Crakett is, or so Sebastian believes, his secret weapon to safeguard his painting, whereas he will actually be our secret weapon, because it will be you. Though the man's acute distrust of everyone will prevent him from disclosing the exact location of his hidden painting, he will install Crakett, *you*, nearby to guard it. When you are left alone, you will use your burglary skills to seek out its hiding place, steal it and stash the painting, which should be rolled up and not in a frame, in the secret compartment cunningly fashioned in your hump. As a surprise for his brother, Ebenezer also wants you to replace the painting with another that I strongly suggest, if you value your sanity, you avoid looking at." Butler shivered in revulsion at an image that leapt involuntarily into his thoughts. "You then use your uncanny ability to move about unobserved, leave the castle and return here. You get paid, leave and we never set eyes on each other again." Butler studied Furtive's face for signs of approval. "Well, what do you think?"

"Yer right, it's a good plan, except that yer failed ter mention how I swap places with the hunchback without anyone knowing, and what will the real Crakett be doing while I'm impersonating him."

"The reason I left this detail until last is because it is so cunning I was worried you might faint when you discover how ingenious it is. As soon as Crakett receives word to travel to Castle

Drooge, we will set a trap under the railway bridge situated a little way down the road, which his carriage will have to pass under. On his approach we will release two jets of chloroform from concealed tubes, one at the driver and the other into the carriage. Both men will succumb quickly to the gas and fall asleep. Lurch, hidden a short distance away, will stop the horses. We substitute you for Crakett and temporarily hide them in the bushes with Lurch guarding them. I'll be disguised as a carriage driver and will deliver you to the castle, where you can pretend to be the man Sebastian expects. Though like us, he may have seen a photograph of the hunchback, the two have never met, so there's no fear of him suspecting you are not the real Crakett by your voice, though I do suggest you make it sound a bit hunchbacky.

"And what does a hunchback's voice sound like?"

Butler shrugged. "You'll have to use your imagination. To get back to the plan I have craftily devised. When I have dropped you off at the castle, I will return to pick up Crakett, the driver and Lurch and drive them to a small abandoned cottage on the moors. And so they remain oblivious to what is happening until our mission has been completed, both men will be given a sleeping potion. After you have stolen the painting the carriage will be brought back to the road with the driver and Crakett onboard, revived and sent on their way to the Castle. Yes, obviously they will arrive late and for them it will suddenly be night or early morning, but all involved will be confused by the event and won't have any idea what really took place."

"There's no mistake, it's a cunning scheme right enough. I tell yer Butler, if yer ever turned criminal full time, the world could be yours."

"I'm hoping circumstances never become that dire. After this job, and when Jacobus Drooge's hidden wealth is found, I'll have enough to live as I would like too, though I'm still not certain what that entails yet."

"And I'm guessing being a manservant ter the old geezer ain't part of any particular future of yours yer decide on?"

"It most certainly is not. Ebenezer will be able to hire all the staff he needs to take care of his whims, if, that is, he can bear to part with the money it would cost."

Furtive took a long suck on his pilfered cigar and blew out a long stream of pungent smoke. "When Crakett turns up at the castle a second time with no recollection of arriving the first time, Sebastian will surely become suspicious and check his painting as soon as he returns home. He'll realize it's stolen and perhaps piece some of the puzzle together."

"I have no doubts he will, but the two brothers are playing a game. It's like chess, each make their move until the winner is decided.

Tonight, that will be Ebenezer. Obviously, Sebastian will be annoyed, but he plays by their strange rules and will accept his defeat ungraciously. Ebenezer would do the same if Sebastian won."

"I'll never understand the likes of people like them. Are you saying Ebenezer don't want his grandpappy's treasure, he just wants ter beat his brother?"

"Oh, he wants it, badly. But defeating his brother is also just as important to him."

Furtive stubbed out the cigar and both men sipped their drinks.

"If you want to take a close look at Castle Drooge, there's a telescope upstairs trained on it. Lurch is keeping a lookout lest Sebastian tries something unexpected."

Furtive placed his empty glass on the table and stood. "Yeah, don't mind if I do. I didn't realize it was so close."

Butler climbed to his feet. "It's only about a quarter mile away."

Furtive followed Butler from the room and up the grand staircase. When they reached the top, a scream rang out.

With a concerned expression, Butler faced the bathroom door. "That was Ebenezer!"

Furtive giggled. "I guess he found the surprise I left for him in his toilet."

Butler looked at the burglar with a disgusted expression. "You didn't... you know... in his personal toilet?"

Furtive grinned and shook his head. "Nothing like that. I just relocated that surprise he left for me in the safe."

"You put the jack in the box in his toilet?"

"I guess I kinda did, and by his scream I assume he found it."

"BUTLER!"

Butler sighed. "I take it you can find your own way to the telescope room while I sort this out."

"Not a problem." Humming a cheerful tune, Furtive walked away.

Butler approached the bathroom door and knocked. "It's Butler, Sir. Are you dressed, because I'm not coming in if you are naked." He shivered with revulsion at the thought.

"No, I am not damn well dressed; I just got out of the bath and was about to use the toilet when that thing I put in the safe to surprise Furtive, leapt out at me."

"Please, Sir, at least cover those private bits of yours with a towel or something."

A scuffling sound and then Ebenezer's voice, "Okay, my privates are covered."

Butler entered and quickly averted his eyes. "Oh my god! Couldn't you have found something a little larger, Sir? That face flannel barely covers half of it!"

"Just get in here and help me to my feet, this floor's freezing my bum off; its already gone so numb I think you'll have to rub both cheeks to bring the circulation back. And shut that damn door, you're letting in a draft."

Butler sighed, entered and shut the door.

6th
CHAPTER

CRAKETT MURDERSIN

The room, lit by a single candle on the mantle above the hearth, was mostly shadow. The hunched silhouette form of Crakett Murdersin stood at the window, peering out at the rooftops and gas lit streets of grimy Whitechapel. An occasional scream pierced the cool night air as someone was robbed, beaten, murdered or all three. Running feet on cobbles, barking dogs, screeching cats, tuneless drunkards singing and music from the inn's bar on the ground floor, were the comforting night sounds of Whitechapel's crime-choked streets.

Footsteps much closer than those in the street below made by a robber rapidly fleeing from his victim who shouted for the thief to stop, which obviously he had no intent of doing, approached Crakett's room and paused outside the door.

Two raps of the visitor's knuckles upon the timber door were followed by the innkeeper's voice, "Mr. Murdersin, another telegram for you has arrived."

Crakett ignored the man and continued to stare out of the window.

"I'll just slide it under the door, shall I?"

A few moments later an envelope was thrust under the door and the innkeeper's footsteps faded down the hall.

A turn of Crakett's head brought the envelope under his scrutiny. Even from this distance and in the dim light he could detect the dampness staining the paper. He shook his head in dismay and went to retrieve the message. It was, as he expected, from Sebastian. He turned it over. The knife the innkeeper had used to peel back the gummed edge he had steamed open, must have been blunter than his trusty fruit knife. Normally, anyone tampering with anything of his would suffer his wrath, but in this instance Crakett was unconcerned his messages were read by another who should not. When he had first realized his correspondence was being intercepted—which, due to the innkeeper's inadequacy in such matters, made it as obvious as an elephant hiding amongst a flock of sheep—he knew only one man could have bribed the innkeeper to do so, Ebenezer Drooge. Though Crakett had played a few scenarios in his head, only one stood out, that it was important for Ebenezer to discover when he would travel to Sebastian's castle. Though without further information he was unable to fathom the full details of Ebenezer's scheme, he had taken certain precautions to guard against one he thought most likely. He pulled back the damp flap and slipped the telegram from inside. Ignoring the innkeeper's dirty thumb print, he read the message.

Crakett. Important you arrive here December 24th. E is planning something. He has services of burglar now. I have extra men in castle and watching E's house. S.D

Crakett placed the message in the candle flame and dropped the burning paper into the fire grate. He had arrangements to make. He walked to the window and slid up the sash. A draft of air tainted with the foul stench of Whitechapel's inhabitants, and much more, entered, swirled round the room and with a gleeful howl extinguished the candle flame. Crakett leapt through the opening. A cat seeking refuge on the lower roof from a prowling pack of mangy street dogs, screeched in surprise when a slightly less dark shadow suddenly landed nearby and just as quickly disappeared across the rooftops.

7th CHAPTER

CUNNING PLAN GLITCH

It **had not** been difficult to avoid
Sebastian's guards to get away from the house
and carry out the first stage of Butler's cunning
plan. Dressed in the guise of a carriage driver,
Butler stood on the railway track with a pair of
binoculars aimed along the road that led beneath
the bridge. He focused in on the approaching
carriage. Though the passenger's identity was
impossible to distinguish encased within the
carriage's gloomy interior, Butler was confident it
was Crakett Murdersin. The telegram he had
received from the Whitechapel innkeeper had
informed him Crakett would arrive today. The
road only led to the Drooge estate and was so
infrequently travelled it could be no one else. He
slithered down the steep grassy embankment to
where Furtive, disguised as the hunchback,
crouched concealed in the bushes beside one of
the two bellows filled with chloroform gas. Tubes
fixed to the two nozzles led into the tunnel and
had been fixed to the brick wall. To disguise
them, Butler had painted the tubes to match the

brickwork, making them almost indiscernible from their immediate surroundings.

"He's coming," Butler informed Furtive. Again, he was impressed by the man's disguise. If Crakett hadn't changed significantly from his photograph, no one would be able to tell he wasn't the man he impersonated. "Don't operate the bellow until the front two horses emerge from the tunnel."

"Aye captain, I knows what ter do. Yer told me enough times. Arrr! That yer did."

Butler's expression changed to puzzlement when he looked at Furtive. "Why are you talking like that?"

"Arrr! Talk like what, captain?"

"Talking like a pirate?"

"It's not a pirate," replied Furtive in his normal voice. "I'm talking like a hunchback."

Butler's eyebrows were up again. "If Crakett or any hunchback not aboard a ship flying the Jolly Rodger talks like that, I'll clean your teeth with my tongue."

"Oh, yer that certain are yer?"

"I am."

"Alright," mumbled Furtive a little sulkily, "I'll try summink different."

"I think that will be best." To warn Lurch the carriage was coming, Butler signalled him with a wave of his arms.

Lurch, who waited a short way along the track, waved a thick arm in reply and then did his best to hide his large form amongst the bushes beside the track far too small to conceal his bulk completely.

Butler crouched and with his gaze joining Furtive's upon the tunnel exit, gripped the handles of the bellows and waited.

It wasn't long before the pounding of hooves on the dusty dirt road was heard and changed to an echoing tempo when they entered the short tunnel. The two lead horses snorted as they emerged once more into daylight.

"Now!" whispered Butler, urgently.

Together the men pressed the bellow handles together. At great speed chloroform fumes were forced along the tubes. Furtive's, having a slightly shorter journey and set at a greater height, was first to release its sleep-inducing gas. It burst from the nozzle to form a cloud of vapor that enveloped the driver.

Butler's tube emitted its gas in a similar fashion a second later. The whoosh of fumes entered the carriage's passenger department.

The hunchback was not enjoying the ride. The coach swayed with every bump the hard wheels bounced over. Nausea had kept him company for a while now and he wasn't sure how much longer he could prevent his breakfast of ham, greasy eggs and potatoes from making an unwelcome appearance.

He poked his head out of the window, glad of the cool wind upon his clammy face, and shouted at the driver. "Can't you avoid at least one bump or rut during this hellish journey?"

The driver turned to look at his slightly green passenger. "Sorry, Mr. Murdersin, the track is nothing but bumps, so trying to avoid them is something impossible."

A particularly large rut the driver failed to avoid, bounced Crakett into the air. His head slammed against the door frame and his stomach lurched something awful. He forced the lumpy bile back down his throat and glared at the driver. "Damn you man! At least make an effort to avoid the worst of them."

"I'm not sure they ain't all as bad as each other, but if you think you can do a better job yer welcome to swap places. I'd like nothing more than to relax in there all comfy like for a change. It has to be better than being bounced all over the place on this damn seat, what seems to have been designed to extract as much pain and discomfort from my bum as humanly possible."

Sensing the immediate re-emergence of his greasy breakfast, Crakett slouched back in his seat and took a few deep breaths. Bounced from side to side, up and down and every other possible direction, he glanced around the carriage interior, which he now looked upon as his own personal torture chamber. He would be glad when the torturous journey reached its end; he wasn't looking forward to the return trip, perhaps he'd walk. Two bumps in quick succession from opposite sides of the track swayed the coach violently. His breakfast seized its chance to escape, gave a whoop of delight and sped at amazing speed up its host's throat.

The hunchback felt its imminent arrival and aware this time there would be no stopping it, he dived for the open window to set it free. The force of his body slamming against the flimsy door was more than the feeble, worn catch could resist. It flew open taking the passenger with it. With a plume of vomit spaying from his mouth, the hunchback fell to the ground, rolled down a slight incline that suddenly became a lot steeper. Bushes and thorny scrub snatched at him, but failed to halt his plummet. That event happened when he reached the bottom and his head struck something hard. Dazed, he lay there and gazed up at the blue sky gradually taken from his sight by rolling grey clouds. Rain was coming. He slipped into unconsciousness.

The carriage door, now free of the weight of its unwelcome passenger and propelled by a large bump the recently evicted traveller was lucky to have missed, slammed shut.

The driver felt, more than heard, the sound of the closing door. He glanced back, spying nothing amiss he returned his gaze upon the approaching railway bridge.

The carriage shot out of the tunnel and after a short distance its driver slump to the side. Lurch stepped out from the bushes but made no attempt to stop the horses.

"Why isn't he stopping it," asked Furtive.

"He will. He doesn't want to scare the horses."

When the rear of the carriage drew level, Lurch reached out and grabbed it. He let the speed of the coach drag him along and gradually dug in his heels, adding two fresh ruts to the bump-ridden track. The struggling horses slowed before coming to a gentle halt.

Butler and Furtive rushed down the bank and along the track.

Wary of the murderous passenger and uncertain if the chloroform had been as successful at knocking out Crakett as it had the driver, Butler told Lurch to check on the hunchback's condition.

Lurch opened the door, almost pulling it from its hinges, and stuck his large head inside.

The confused look upon his face when he looked at Butler, though not an unusual expression, in this instance caused Butler concern. "What is it, Lurch?"

"It's empty."

Butler rushed forward and looked inside. Lurch was right. It was as empty as a fresh grave in a cemetery favoured by body snatchers.

Something was wrong, very wrong. He glanced back along the track, but saw no sign of the missing hunchback. *Maybe he wasn't on board, but if not, what was the carriage doing here? Both Ebenezer and Sebastian had their own transport to take them to the ball tonight, so that couldn't be the reason.* He turned to Lurch. "Bring me the driver."

Lurch reached up and plucked the unconscious man from his uncomfortable seat and placed him on the ground beside Butler.

Butler pulled a small bottle of smelling salts from his pocket and told the hunchback disguised Furtive to hide for a moment. Once Furtive had moved around to the far side of the coach, Butler waved the smelling salts under the driver's nose.

It took the man a few moments to awake. His drowsy eyes focused at Butler. "Who are you?"

"That is of no importance. Where's your passenger?"

"Mr. Murdersin?"

"Yes! Where is he?"

The driver tilted his head to look up at the carriage door. "He's inside of course. I did give 'im the opportunity to swop..."

"He isn't. The carriage is empty."

"Impossible; I spoke to the strange fellow shortly before we passed under the bridge. He was feeling a little queer. Green as a toad he was."

Butler stood, told Lurch to watch the driver and moved around the carriage to talk with Furtive.

"So...?" questioned Furtive.

"The driver said Crakett was on board; he spoke to him shortly before the bridge and that he looked a bit sickly. I'm thinking he either jumped out for some reason or fell out."

"Yer reckon he's somewhere back along the track?"

Butler nodded. "We have to decide whether we continue with the plan with a few minor changes, or cancel it?"

"Yer got that ball tonight, which will be another year for it comes around again, and I don't think Sebastian will halt his plans just because yer ain't ready with yours."

Butler remained deep in thought for a few moments. "We'll go ahead. Working for Ebenezer for another year is not something I am willing to endure; it's now or not at all. Now the driver's awake, he can take you to Castle Drooge. Tell him you fell out. Lurch and I will go look for Crakett; he shouldn't be hard to find, and take him to the cottage as planned."

"Sounds good ter me."

Butler followed Furtive around to the driver.

"Look, there he is!" said the driver on spying the hunchback. "What happened, yer fall out did yer."

Furtive ignored the man. "Come on, let's get this thing moving. I'm already late." He climbed into the carriage.

Lurch helped the driver to his feet.

"He's not the most sociable passenger I ever had," moaned the driver, "and probably a lousy tipper knowing my luck. He did look a bit better though, his greenness ain't there now and he sounds a bit different. Chucked his guts up I expect."

Furtive poked his head out of the window. "If you want any tip at all, lousy or otherwise, yer better climb aboard and get this damn thing moving."

The driver dobbed his cap to the passenger. "Yes, Sir, climbing aboard now, Sir." He climbed aboard and grabbed the reigns. He glanced down at Butler and Lurch. "You two wanna lift somewhere?"

"No they damn well don't," said Furtive.

The driver rolled his eyes. "Starting the horses now, Sir. Soon 'ave yer at yer destination." He nodded goodbye to the two men watching him and with a swish of the reigns, clucked the horses into motion.

Butler turned to Lurch. "Come big feller, we have a missing hunchback to track down."

Lurch followed Butler along the track and under the bridge.

8th CHAPTER

CASTLE DROOGE

The **carriage crossed** the drawbridge spanning the foul smelling, stagnant moat, passed under the raised portcullis, through the opening normally blocked by two thick oak gates covered in bands of iron, and clattered across the bone-shaking cobbled courtyard of Castle Drooge. The guards posted around the ramparts scrutinized the carriage as it came to a rattling stop in front of the main door to the inner building.

Flint emerged through the inner castle's main entrance, hurried over to the carriage, opened the door and smiled a little nervously at its lone passenger. "Welcome to Castle Drooge, Mr. Murdersin."

With an expression of moody disinterest, Furtive stared at the man, but said not a word.

Made nervous by the hunchback's piercing stare, lack of speech and his infamous reputation with a fruit knife, Flint said, "Mr. Sebastian Drooge is waiting for you in his library, Sir." He stood back and held the door open. When the man failed to disembark, he nervously peered inside. The carriage was empty. Puzzled by the hunchback's sudden disappearance, he turned. A surprised screech escaped from his lips at the unexpected sight of the missing guest standing beside him. Eager to be free of the disturbing man, Flint stepped around him. "Please follow me, Mr. Murdersin." He headed for the door. After a few steps he paused to check the soles of his shoes and seemed surprised to find them lacking the foul substance he expected to discover there.

Furtive cast his gaze around the courtyard. He counted three men, but there might be more not in his view and maybe others posted inside. The door was closed behind him after he had stepped through.

Ebenezer was angry. "What do you mean you couldn't find him?"

"Sorry, Sir, I thought I had stated it plainly enough. He wasn't to be found, not there, gone, vanished from the face of the earth..."

"That's enough, Butler. You know how important this is to me. What in hell's name could have happened to him?"

"We did find a faint trail of crushed grass leading to the drop into the quarry, Sir, but I saw no sign of him below. If he has fallen over the edge there is a good chance it resulted in his death; it's a long way down."

"I'd rather know for certain one way or the other, but if he fell into the quarry and survived the fall, Diablo will get him for sure."

Butler grimaced. "A gruesome, horrible death, Sir, and probably quite a bit of pain and suffering involved as well. Not a nice way to meet your maker."

"I wouldn't feel sorry for him. I imagine all those who have died at his hands would have thought their deaths were just as horrid, especially if that blunt fruit knife of his was the cause. What concerns me is that if on the slim chance he does survive and turns up at the castle, two identical hunchbacks claiming to be the same person are going to cause a bit of a problem, don't you think?"

"I am afraid it's a chance we'll have to risk, Sir. Time constraints prevent us from doing anything about it. If we had more men, like I suggested..."

"Oh! It's my fault your perfect plan is falling apart at the seams, is it?"

"I did say there might be complications we couldn't foresee."

"Complications! Damn it, Butler, your whole plan revolves around Furtive being accepted by my brother as the real Crakett Murdersin, something that will fail miserably if the real Crakett turns up."

"Well, Sir, it's too late to back out now, Furtive's already inside Sebastian's castle. I suggest you trot off to the ball and leave me to worry about things here. There is still a very good chance Furtive will find the painting and remove himself from the castle before the real Crakett, if he's not dead, knocks on the Sebastian's door."

"Let's hope you're right, Butler. I've waited a long time to get one over on my brother and find Jacobus's inheritance. There have been too many disappointments and to face another when I feel we are so close might be the end of me."

"No need for such talk, Sir. You may look as weak as a politician's resolve when a bribe is on offer, but you have the heart of an ox and the stamina of a racing horse. Come, Sir, your carriage awaits. If you are ready, I'll drive you to Havasham Hall."

Ebenezer took one last look in the mirror. The black jacket and trousers, white shirt and bow tie, which he only wore for the ball, seemed to sag more on his thin frame every year. He stood as straight as his crooked back would allow, placed the top hat on his head, gripped the ebony cane in his right hand and turned to look at his man servant. "I'm ready as I'll ever be."

"You actually look quite dashing in your formal attire, Sir. Maybe a lady will take a fancy to you tonight and you to her. It would be pleasant company in your old age if you could convince her to marry you."

Ebenezer perked up. "You really think so?"

"Yes, Sir, I do. If I was a single female of about your age, so close to the grave, I'd snatch you up real quick."

"Thank you, Butler. I think that's one of the nicest things anyone has said to me that did not involve a profitable cash transaction."

"Stop it, Sir, or you'll bring a tear to my eye." Butler smiled warmly at his employer, turned to one side and crooked his arm. "Sir, may I please have the honour of escorting you to your carriage?"

"Yes, Butler, you may." Ebenezer linked his skeletal arm through Butler's.

Butler caught a whiff of something. "New cologne, Sir?"

"No, an old one I used to splash on in my younger days. It's called Stallion."

"Horses certainly sprang to mind when it assaulted my nose, Sir."

Arm in arm, they left the room.

Furtive, already impressed by the castle's grand and foreboding exterior, was even more so with its interior. He had expected it to be cold, dank and musty like his brother's manor, but it wasn't. The stone walls of the passage he currently passed through were adorned with tapestries and paintings. Vases and figurines stood atop small tables positioned at intervals—the man obviously employed no one as clumsy as Lurch or there would be piles of broken china and splintered wood.

Flint paused at an arched, oak door, knocked, opened it and announced his guest. "Sir, Mr. Murdersin is here to see you."

When he noticed the puzzled frown form on his employer's face and his peering look through the opening, Flint turned. There was no sign of the hunchback. He huffed. "I wish he'd stop doing that."

"You have an impressive castle, Sebastian."

Both heads turned toward the voice. Their guest sat in a relaxed manner in one of the large armchairs. In one hand a glass of whiskey and in the other a fat cigar."

Flint was stunned. "But...how..."

Sebastian was impressed and smiled. "That will be all, Flint."

"Yes, Sir." Flint cast a nervous glance at the hunchback, backed out of the room and closed the door.

"That was impressive, Mr. Murdersin," praised Sebastian admirably, "and without making a sound. It confirms what I already knew; you are the right man for the job."

Furtive shrugged casually. "It is a skill that has come in handy on many occasions."

Sebastian headed for the whisky decanter to pour himself a drink, but halted when his guest spoke.

"I took the liberty of pouring you one before I sat down." His smoking cigar pointed at the glass. "It's on the table there."

Sebastian glanced at the drink and smiled. "Amazing! Is it possible you could teach me that trick?"

"Trick!" Furtive slammed his glass on the low table and rose to his feet. "A trick! Well, Sir, if that is what you think I am, a simple carnival magician, I see my talents are not required here. I will remove myself from your castle forthwith."

"No, please don't, Mr. Murdersin. I am sorry, I meant no offence. Obviously it's not a trick but a great skill. You must understand Mr. Murdersin; people like me rarely witness talents like those you have so expertly displayed. All we have to compare them to is fantastical magic tricks. Please, Sir, forgive me?"

Furtive, content he had put the man on the defensive, the reason for his feigned outburst, returned the glass to his hand and resumed his seat. "I accept your apology, Sebastian, and you must forgive me also. Perhaps I reacted a little harshly. I blame that long uncomfortable carriage ride from the train station. Traveling along some of those roads is a living hell."

"I assure you there is nothing to forgive, it was my mistake." Sebastian sat down in an opposing arm chair and took a large gulp of whisky.

Furtive gave a causal wave of his hand to dismiss the matter. "It is already forgotten."

Sebastian tried his hardest not to stare at the wad of hot cigar ash that had fallen on to the chair's arm. The scorch mark it would leave in the one-hundred-year-old fabric would not be forgotten so easily.

Furtive took another sip of his drink and smacked his lips in appreciation. "So, Sebastian, what is the full nature of the job you require of me."

Unable to drag his eyes away from the lengthening protrusion of cigar ash forming as his guest took a long drag, Sebastian explained. "It's a protection job. My brother, who lives in yonder manor..."

"That must be the building I noticed from the road; dreary looking place in desperate need of maintenance."

Sebastian nodded, wondering how the finger length of ash on his guest's cigar was managing to sustain its grip. "Yes, that would be it." He casually leaned forward and pushed the cut crystal ashtray toward the hunchback. "If you run out of room for your ash on the chair's arm, please, feel free to use the ashtray."

Furtive smirked as his eyes flicked from the cigar to the ashtray. His thumb flicked the end of the cigar, sending the ash missile into the air.

Sebastian glanced at the airborne ash, the ashtray and his expensive hand-woven Turkish rug between them. It was almost more than Sebastian could do to prevent himself from diving for it. His anxious eyes followed the ash's arc through the air. When it was above the ashtray it collapsed into a snowfall of grey flecks that drifted into the vessel designed to catch them.

Before he knew that he was doing it, Sebastian leapt to his feet and began clapping. "Bravo!" When he realized he was, he blushed. He abruptly stopped and resumed his seat. He composed himself and continued. "As I was saying, my brother and I each own one painting from a pair and I am very eager to bring them back together. I plan to steal his painting tonight and he will, I believe, attempt to steal mine at the same time. It is this painting of mine I want you to protect, to ensure he doesn't get his grubby, miserly hands on it."

"A simple task of which I can guarantee a satisfactory result. I sense your motivation for having the two reunited is not that normally inspired by an art collector's temperament. I am curious, what is the significance of the two paintings to drive your obvious determination to steal your brother's?"

"Each painting contains a set of clues leading to a family keepsake, a worthless family heirloom, a knick-knack, nothing more and certainly something of no financial importance, but something we both desire nevertheless. Only when the two paintings are together are the clues decipherable, something we both only realized a few years ago. Ever since we have played a sort of game where we each attempt to steal the other's painting. I fear the winning has now become more important than the reward."

"Interesting." While he thought about what he had just heard, Furtive took another sip of whisky and another puff on the cigar. *Ebenezer told him the clues in the paintings would lead to a vast wealth, and Sebastian, nothing of any great wealth; one of the brothers was lying.* "I gather there is no chance of you two combining your resources to find this... *worthless family heirloom, a knick-knack, nothing more.*"

Sebastian shook his head. "I am afraid that point has passed a long time ago. We have never been close; there has always been a sibling rivalry between us, which has festered over the years into a septic wound now impossible to heal."

Sebastian glanced at the mantle clock. "It will soon be time for me to leave. I have a luncheon to attend before the ball, so I'll show you to the room I require you to guard."

On his journey into the deepest bowels of the castle, Furtive memorized every twist, turn, door and staircase. Though the guards posted in the house had so far been few, when his host paused at a door, rapped out a special code and called out a password, he sensed that was about to change. The door was promptly unlocked and opened. The revealed corridor was lined with two rows of four men; all had their gaze fixed upon the hunchback and all held a weapon. He followed Sebastian through the door that was immediately locked as soon as they had passed through, and along the corridor. The guard's eyes followed his progress between them. They paused at a similar door at the far end. After Sebastian had unlocked the door with the key taken from his pocket, they stepped into a small room.

While Sebastian relocked the door, Furtive glanced around the small chamber. It was lit by a single flickering candle set in a bracket on one of the stone walls. The completely empty room had only one door, the one they had just entered through.

"I am surprised you require my services, Sebastian. Your security seems sufficiently robust to ward off any thief who has a notion to steal that which you obviously treasure."

"Normally, I would agree with you, but a short while ago Ebenezer's butler contacted a burglar with apparently extraordinary skills in the thieving department. His name is Furtive

Freddy. A silly name I know, but he probably believes it sounds cool. It adds credence to the other information I was supplied with, that he is not the brightest of people."

Furtive gritted his teeth against the slur. "Really, I have actually heard something of this man. Like you, I've heard say he is very good at his job, an expert thief and one much admired in my circle of thievery and murderous deeds. Against his intelligence I have heard no insult."

"Oh, yes, apparently, he couldn't hit the floor if he fell on it, and would lose a debate with a door knob, and let me see, what else, oh yes..."

"I've heard enough," said Furtive gruffly. He gazed around the bare chamber. "Is this the room you want me to guard?"

"It is not." Sebastian walked to the far side and shielding his actions with his body, pressed a series of stone blocks in the wall.

The muffled sounds of clanking chains were followed by the louder grinding of stone. Furtive watched in amazement as the wall on his right pivoted open to reveal stone steps spiralling down. "The room I want you to protect is down there."

Brackets fixed just inside the passage held torches. Sebastian grabbed one and held the tip over the candle flame. The oil soaked rags wrapped around the end burst into flame. He turned to face Furtive. "Follow me." Sebastian stepped through the opening and climbed down the stairs.

Furtive followed.

The stone staircase illuminated by an occasional candle Sebastian lit during his descent, wound down through the rock a considerable depth before reaching bottom. Furtive stepped into the long chamber and watched his host move along its length lighting the three-candelabra positioned in the room. The flickering light enabled Furtive to examine the room's details. Though the floor had been laid with smooth stone slabs, the walls were rough and arched, a natural cavern. Stalactites of various thicknesses and lengths hung from the roof like a natural chandelier. Furtive stepped farther into the room and examined the contents of the glass-topped cabinets lining each wall. His eyes roamed over displays of numerous different objects that obviously held some value to their owner. Some held books, open at pages adorned with archaic symbols and pictures that hinted heavily toward the occult. Others contained ancient documents, strange artefacts, rings, bracelets, amulets, grotesque figurines and shrunken heads; in fact, the whole collection seemed to be biased toward the macabre and was a clue to their owner's personality.

With a sizzle of speedily quenched flames, Sebastian extinguished the torch in a bucket of water beside the staircase and turned to face his guest. "Well, Mr. Murdersin, what do you think of my wonderful collection?"

"I am afraid, Sebastian, they remain as much a mystery to me as my unfathomable talents do to you, but saying that, they are impressive, though I see no sign of the painting you wish me to guard."

"That is because it has been well concealed. All you need to know is it's here. The only entrance to the room is via the staircase, which can only be accessed through the secret door I alone know the correct sequence of blocks to press to gain access. This in turn is protected by the locked doors at each end of a corridor packed with armed guards. To access the guard-filled passage, as you witnessed me do earlier, a special knock and password must be given, something which I change each time I visit this room. So, you see, though it is unlikely anyone will disturb you, if someone other than me comes down those stairs, you can be assured their intention is to steal. On my return I will call out a password before descending..." he paused to think of one. "The password will be Rumpelstiltskin!"

Furtive raised his bushy glued on eyebrows. "Rumpelstiltskin?"

"Yes, the name no one could guess." Sebastian glanced at Furtive. Will you be using your fruit knife if an unwelcome visitor does make an appearance?"

Furtive shrugged. "Maybe, but it is not the only weapon I bring into service." His hand moved so fast it was a blur and though Sebastian had no idea where the hunchback had concealed such a thing, it now pointed directly at him. "Sometimes I use this. It's a four-barrelled blunderbuss I call *Daisy.*"

Sebastian stared down the four tubes of doom and gulped fearfully. "*Daisy?*" he croaked.

Furtive grinned. "Only kidding. Sorry, it's my assassin's sense of fun. Its real name is *Grave Filler.*"

"Well, Sir, that certainly is catchier," Sebastian said anxiously. "Stuck under my nose like it is, I am certainly receiving an image of my grave, which I imagine anyone faced with such a fearsome weapon in a threatening manner, like it is now at me, would gladly jump into to avoid the deadly repercussions when the trigger is pulled."

"It's okay, Sebastian, even though it has a sensitive trigger, the safety is on..." He glanced along the side of the weapon. "Oops, silly me, no it isn't, this model doesn't have one." He pointed the weapon away from his host. "That was risky. You are a lucky man, Sebastian, a single twitch of my finger and, BOOM! your brains would have been on display around the room like all your macabre artefacts."

Sebastian gulped. "Unlike my underpants, I certainly feel lucky, Mr. Murdersin." His shaking finger pointed to the far end of the room where a small lounge area had been set out. "As you can see, you will be quite comfortable down here. There are snacks, whiskey and cigars," he walked forward, picked up the ashtray from the low table and placed it on the arm of the single comfy chair, "and for your convenience, an ashtray. The hearth has been laid ready for you to light if you get chilly."

Furtive glanced at the stone fireplace located on one side. "Where does the smoke go?"

"Luckily, there was a natural fissure in the rock I could tap into." Sebastian's gaze flicked to the mantle clock. "I must leave you as I am already running late and due to a certain recent event, a particular piece of my attire desperately needs to be changed. I will lock all access points behind me and return in the morning, sooner if anyone attempts to rob me. Now, Mr. Murdersin, do you have any questions before I hurriedly leave?"

Furtive shook his head. "About my responsibility here, you have covered every eventuality in such exact detail I am confident the very next person I see climb down those stairs will be you. This, I think, will turn out to be the easiest job I have ever undertaken. However, another related question springs to my lips, if I am guarding your painting, who will steal your brother's."

"An astute question, Mr. Murdersin. I have employed another to complete that task who goes by the name of, *Shadow*!"

Furtive scoffed. "The Shadow is just a myth, nothing more than a legend."

"Well, Mr. Murdersin, myth or not, tonight Shadow will steal Ebenezer's painting and bring it to me. I will return at dawn. Goodbye Mr. Murdersin." With a strained walk, Sebastian headed for the staircase.

Furtive heard the wall at the top grind back into place and then silence. To check the man had really gone, he moved to the staircase and listened. All was silent. He moved to the far end of the room, laid Grave Filler on the table, poured a whisky, lit a cigar, reclined in the comfortable armchair and thought about what he had just heard. If Shadow existed, as Sebastian confidently asserted, and if the stories I've heard about him are true, and his mission was to obtain the painting, then it was a certainty the phantom thief would succeed. It's vital I find Sebastian's painting and exit the castle as quickly as possible, so I can warn Butler. As well as a thief, Shadow was also a ruthless assassin. Anyone unlucky enough to become between Shadow and his assignment, would likely be killed!

Sebastian's employment of Shadow, and no doubt Crakett's similar high fee, confirmed what I already thought to be true, Sebastian had lied, and the paintings led to something a lot more valuable than a family heirloom of little worth.

Furtive gazed around the room as he contemplated the hiding place of Sebastian's painting.

Drops of rain spattered onto the unconscious hunchback's face. Slowly he opened his eyes and gazed at the dark, moody sky high above. Grateful his sickness had fled, but less so for the horrible taste in his mouth; he climbed to his feet and surveyed his surroundings. Lit by the dimness of sunset fast approaching, it was an indication he had been unconscious for a few hours. He gazed up the un-climbable side of the steep cliff. The broken branches of bushes and flattened shrub that marked his recent passage of descent, made him realize how lucky he had been not to have suffered any serious injury or worse. From the tool marks etched in the rock all around him, he guessed he had fallen into a disused quarry. Unsure of which direction led to Castle Drooge, he chose one at random and headed off through the quarry.

Diablo stirred from a deep slumber. Its long hairy snout opened in a wide yawn that revealed every one of the sharp yellow teeth lining its powerful jaws. Claw-tipped paws stretched out to ease the stiffness of sleep. Eyelids flicked up to expose pupils as black as death floating in pools of evil red. Its nose twitched. Its head lifted. It drew into its flared nostrils the breeze wafting through the passage. The taint of human was in the air. A large pink tongue flicked over eager teeth in anticipation of the approaching meal. It had not tasted human for so long it had forgotten how good it tasted. With eagerness to refuel that memory, Diablo climbed to its feet and slunk toward the entrance of its lair.

9th
CHAPTER

SHADOW

With a mysterious name like Shadow, it is taken for granted that its namesake would not be wearing anything white or brightly coloured. Shadow's attire conformed to this assumption and was of the dark variety. So dark in fact, actual shadows were jealous. Accessorizing the dark clothes covering the figure from hooded head to black-booted toes, was a facemask as black as moonless midnight, that completed the rationale behind the assassin thief's slightly creepy nom-de-plume. Belts, buttons and buckles, of which there were many—black naturally—were dull and would reflect no light to inform anyone who might happen to look in the assassin thief's direction that there was anyone there. An array of black-handled blades were arranged in positions of easy access over the slim black form. All had bright, finely-honed blades, but by the time anyone was unfortunate enough to have noticed the glint of the weapon, they were already dead.

Shadow, though hard to distinguish from the slightly lighter shadows the silent form moved through, was currently crossing through the grounds of Drooge Manor. So furtive were Shadow's creeping skills, Furtive Freddy would have paused in amazement and observed in the hope of learning something new. So light and stealthy was Shadow's progress, not a blade of grass was disturbed in passing. Insects and creatures of the night failed to witness the dark presence. A bat on the hunt for the aforementioned insects. sent out its sonar and dismissed Shadow's feedback as a glitch. The men employed by Sebastian to observe the comings and goings of Drooge Manor, received no hint of the intruder's presence, even when Shadow took a brief rest beside one of them, slipped the man's lunch from his pocket and picked out a cookie before returning the pilfered items. The stolen cookie Shadow nibbled on proved to be stale and was sprinkled on the man's head in retaliation.

Shadow made a complete circuit of the large house before pausing at the front entrance. Though a few entry points that would allow access to the house undetected had been discovered during the detailed reconnoitre, the assassin-thief decided on a more direct access point. A black gloved finger reached for the bell push.

Butler and Lurch were in Ebenezer's study going over their part of the plan. Having just explained to Lurch what he had to do for the tenth time, it was something Butler was finding a little frustrating. "Okay Lurch, so you are sure you now know what you have to do?"

Lurch nodded none too convincingly. "Yes, Mr. Butler, I think I certainly have it all in my head now."

TRING! TRING!

Butler's eyes flicked through the open doorway and across the hallway to settle on the front door. Drooge Manor rarely had visitors at any time of the year, but to have a caller tonight when the two brother's shenanigans were at their peak, raised his hackles of suspicion to a new height.

Butler grabbed the blunderbuss pistol from the table. "Go and see who that is Lurch, but keep your eyes open."

Lurch looked at Butler strangely. "I usually do when I answer the door, Mr. Butler."

"That' good, and whatever you do, don't let anyone in unless I say it's okay."

"Yes, Sir, I understand." Lurch lurched out of the room and across the hall.

Butler hid to one side of the study door and listened to the front door creak open.

Lurch was surprised to see no one standing there. He leaned forward and looked left and right. He straightened and turned his head. "There's no one here, Mr. Butler."

Butler's head appeared round the door frame, his eyes roamed the hall suspiciously. "Close the door."

Lurch closed the door and with an impressed expression, watched when Butler sprung from the study with the pistol held in a two-handed grip and searchingly did a sweep of the hall.

Noticing a white strand of hair on Butler's shoulder, Shadow plucked it off as he passed and let it drift to the ground. By the time it landed gently on the floor, Shadow was in another part of the house.

Butler sensed something amiss. "I don't like it, Lurch."

"What is it you don't like, Sir?"

The door bell ringing and no one there. I don't like it; something's up."

"You think it might have been a trick, Sir?"

"I'm sure it was, perhaps a distraction. Let's double check all the rooms, we'll start downstairs and work our way up. Check every window and door is securely locked and look for anything suspicious or out of place."

"Sorry, Sir, but what happens after double checking every room, my mind sort of went a bit adrift after that?"

Butler sighed. "Follow me and do as I do, and you don't have to keep calling me, *Sir* or *Mr. Butler*, just Butler is fine."

"Okay, Mr. Butler, Sir, I'll try and remember that."

Butler, with little confidence that Lurch would, crouched slightly with the gun held out in front in a double-handed grip and entered the closest room to the front door.

Lurch, keen to follow Butler's instructions as closely as he was able, achieved a similar stance, clasped his hands in front and using pointed fingers to mimic the weapon, followed Butler into the room.

Diablo crouched at the entrance to its lair set into the side of the quarry and watched the strange human below walk by. Though different from any other human it had seen, which to be fair wasn't many, it had been a very long time since anyone had dared to venture into the quarry, it was encouraged by the amount of meat on display. The big lump on its back seemed especially tender and tasty. A tongue flicked out to lap up the drool escaping from its teeth-filled mouth. Silently, it slithered along the track cut into the rock and careful not to alert its dinner that it was on the menu, Diablo climbed down toward it.

From his position in the armchair, Furtive's eyes had surveyed the whole room. Every nook, cranny, fissure and object had been scrutinized. With very few hiding places available, he had reached the conclusion something the size of the rolled painting could only be hidden in one place.

He tilted his head to examine the stalactites. His burglar senses tingled. One of them was not what it seemed. He stubbed out the cigar in the ashtray, something Sebastian would be thankful for, drained the last of the excellent whiskey from his glass and climbed to his feet. He moved over to the desk against the wall, grabbed the back of the antique chair and dragged it beneath the stalactite that held his interest. He climbed on the chair and rapped on the stalactite. A hollow thud rang out. Furtive smiled. After a few moments studying its form, he gripped it with both hands and twisted. It turned. One more twist and it was free. He jumped from the chair, peered into the innards of the hollow stalactite and saw what Ebenezer desperately wanted to get his hands on. He slipped out the painting and laid it on the desk. A hand reached over his shoulder, slipped beneath his coat collar and into the secret compartment of the hollow hump. He pulled out a similar sized rolled painting to the one he had removed and was about to slip it into the hollow stalactite when he remembered Butler's warning not to look at it. Something he promptly ignored. He unrolled the painting and ran his eyes over the artwork. It took his brain a moment to piece all the details together, but when they did it was truly sorry. Furtive's brain had experienced foul, disgusting and horrifying events daily, but this was something much worse and totally unimaginable. Furtive quickly turned his head away, but his eyes, not quite able to believe what they had just witnessed, snuck another peek. Brain, eyes and indeed the owner of both, all thought it was the most horrendous and evil thing they had ever encountered. Furtive quickly rolled it up, stuffed it into the stalactite, climbed onto the chair and fixed it back in position. He returned the chair to the desk, gazed back at the stalactite and shivered. He almost felt sorry for Sebastian.

He snatched Sebastian's painting from the desk and hoping it was more pleasurable to look at than the previous hell spawned image, he nervously unrolled it. Though its dark painted details were not in the least offensive, except perhaps to any artist of merit, the image meant nothing to him and no clues to the whereabouts of the inheritance the two brothers sought jumped out. He rolled it up and carefully slid it into his hump. With a voice so full of smugness it dripped onto the floor, Furtive said, "Step one completed," he then added a smug smile to reinforce his abundance of self-satisfaction.

His next problem would not be so easily resolved.

Even if he managed to open the secret wall door, how was he going to pass through the guard-filled corridor? Electing to handle one problem at a time, he picked up Grave Filler, crossed the room, snatched a candle from a candelabra as he passed and climbed the stairs.

By means of the candlelight, Furtive inspected every inch of the stone walls at the top of the steps. It took his experienced eyes only a few seconds to spot the operating mechanism to open the secret wall door. He pressed his foot against the block near the floor. Clanking and rumbling accompanied the door swinging open. He slipped through and crossed to the wooden door. It was a certainty those in the corridor would have heard the loud rumble and would now be staring at the opposite side of the door. Confident the only key to unlock it was securely secreted in one of Sebastian pockets, he did not waste time knocking but pulled out his lock-picking tools and crouched. A few seconds later the lock gave in to his skilled manipulations. He stood, pocketed his burglar tools and opened the door.

10th CHAPTER

THE THIRD
HUNCHBACK

The guard staring at Drooge Manor, yawned, stamped his feet in an effort to force some warmer blood into his frozen toes and watched the snowflakes drift to the ground. Though the snow was light, he doubted it would remain so and soon heavy snowfall would arrive. At least then he would be able to build a snowman to pass the time. Cold and bored, he wished something would happen to provide him with some excitement.

For the first time in the man's life, his fickle Fairy Godmother listened to her charge and with a sly smirk upon her lips, granted his wish.

It began with a tap on his shoulder. The man turned and staggered two steps back in astonishment. "Why, it's you! Mr. Murdersin." The nervous edge to the man's voice was impossible to miss.

"Yes, it's me."

The guard's hand shot out. "I'm a great fan of your work, Mr. Murdersin, that episode with the fruit knife, legendary."

Crakett glanced at the man's hand. "An enthusiastic admirer you may be, but I see your respect lacks any similar passion. Wasn't a certain finger on that hand a few moments ago shoved so far up your nose it was prodding your eyeball? Don't try to deny it; evidence of said enthusiastic probing still remains firmly attached to the guilty digit."

The guard glanced at the offending finger, retracted the arm and swapped it for his other. "Sorry, Mr. Murdersin, I meant no disrespect, but I assure you no finger of this hand has been anywhere near my nasal cavities."

Crakett glanced at the offered hand before returning his gaze to the man's fearful expression. "And still the disrespect continues. Wasn't that hand a few moments ago stuck down the back of your trousers scratching at something so vigorously I must declare its either part of your body you are trying to remove or something so firmly attached you are wasting your efforts trying to dislodge it?"

The guard whimpered and hid both hands behind his back. "You're going to kill me, aren't you?"

Crakett nodded casually. "Yes, I am."

Another whimper. "Will it be quick?"

Crakett shook his head. "I wouldn't think so."

"Will there be pain?"

"Oh, yes, lots."

The man began to sob.

"Oh, stop that."

"I'll try, Mr. Murdersin, I really will, but it's hard with the thought of my painful death only a few seconds away."

Crakett stared at the man. "Look, you've caught me in a good mood tonight."

Grasping desperately at the hope the hunchback's words invoked, the guard stopped sobbing. "I have?"

"I think so, although that could change at any moment if you don't do exactly as I ask."

"I promise I will, Mr. Murdersin."

"What's your name?"

"Buckley, Sir, Brian Buckley. Are you really not going to kill me?"

Crakett shrugged. "I might not."

So grateful was the man, he fell to his knees. His hands reached out to grasp one of Crakett's to show his appreciation, but froze when he felt the small fruit knife pressed against his throat."

"If any part of your filthy body touches any part of me, including my clothes, this knife will slit you from navel to forehead."

Buckley whimpered and snatched his hands away. His eyes tried to look at the knife blocked from his view by his pointed chin. "Is that *the* fruit knife, Mr. Murdersin?"

Crakett removed it from the man's throat and glanced at it. "It is."

"What an honour it is, Sir, to be almost gruesomely murdered by *the* infamous fruit knife. Did you draw blood, Sir? Please tell me there is blood." Buckley tilted his head back so Crakett could get a better look at his throat.

Dragging his gaze from the view up the man's recently picked hairy nostrils, Crakett glanced at his grimy neck. "Yes, there's a little blood."

Oh, Sir, how can I ever thank you, the lads are going to be soooooo jealous. I hope it never heals."

Crakett sighed.

The happy guard climbed to his feet. "I thought you were working at the castle, Mr. Murdersin?"

"You will find it hard to believe, but I actually am. I am there, and I am here."

Buckley felt the urgent need to scratch his head and did that very thing. Though confused by the cookie crumbs he found there, he had a more immediate problem to occupy his thoughts. "You're right, Sir, I don't understand. I was told you would be staying at the castle all night and if I see anything strange to report in."

Crakett glared at the man. "You think I'm strange?"

"No, Sir, not at all, I swear. I'm making a right mess of this, aren't I? I thought if I ever had the pleasure to meet you it would be something real special, a moment to remember fondly until the day I die."

"It could be short lived enjoyment if you carry on as you are."

"I know, Sir, it's just that I get nervous like. I wish we could start again and forget this dismal embarrassing episode ever occurred."

"A thought that appealed to your parents more than once I should think. Okay, Buckley, here's what we'll do. I want you to go back to the road and keep a watch out for anyone who looks exactly like me coming from the direction of Castle Drooge."

"I'm not sure I understand, Mr. Murdersin. Surely if I see someone who looks exactly like you, it will be you."

"It doesn't matter if you understand or not, you only have to do exactly what I tell you."

"Well...okay. Let's say I see you coming from Castle Drooge, what do I do next?"

"You fire your pistol."

"What, at you!"

"No, Buckley, not at me, because it won't me, just fire it in the air to alert me this imposter is coming. Can you do that, or shall I kill you and find someone who can?"

"No Sir, I'm your man. I'm really grateful fer the opportunity to be working with you, Sir. I won't let you down."

"Make sure you don't, because you know the consequences if you do."

"Indeed I do, Sir. You'll rip me open with yer famous fruit knife and let me just say this Sir, if you do kill me, I can't think of a better way to die than by your hand and with your legendary fruit knife."

"Okay, Buckley, now off you go."

"Yes, Sir, of course, Sir."

Crakett watched Buckley go and then headed for Ebenezer's house.

Butler and Lurch had just completed checking every room in the house, but even though Butler still couldn't shake the feeling that something was wrong, they'd found nothing amiss and no sign of an intruder. They returned to the study.

"I don't like it, Lurch."

"I know, Sir, you already said so."

"No, not just the door bell ringing mysteriously, something is afoot."

"Twelve inches is a foot, Sir."

Butler sighed. "It is, well done, Lurch."

Lurch, pleased by the rareness of being correct, smiled proudly.

"And it's *Butler*, not *Sir*."

"Yes, Sir, I remember you saying."

"I'm going to check outside. You stay here and guard this room. Don't let anyone other than me enter, understood?"

"Yes, Sir. Guard this room and let no one except you enter."

"Good, I'll return shortly." Butler headed for the door, but paused when Lurch asked a question.

"What about Furtive, Sir. Can I let him in?"

"No, Lurch, no one except me."

"Okay, Sir, got it."

Butler took two more steps before he was halted by another question.

"What about Mr. Drooge, Sir, surely I can let him in?"

"No, Lurch, you can't. It may be an imposter who just looks like him. Let no one in. Not the butcher, the baker, the postman or even God himself if he knocks on that door. Let NO ONE through that door. Understand?"

"Oh, yes, Sir, your instructions could not be clearer if you wrote them on a piece of paper and sort of left it on the table there, so I could glance at it every now and again."

Butler lowered his head in dismay. "Shall I write it down for you?"

Lurch nodded. "That might be best, Mr. Butler."

Butler grabbed paper and pen from Ebenezer's desk and wrote his instructions down and placed it on the table where Lurch could read it. "Is it all clear now?"

Lurch glanced at the paper and read it aloud. "Positivity under no circumstances let anyone through the door. Okay, Sir, got it for certain now."

"Good." Butler headed to the door and let out an exasperated breath when Lurch spoke again.

"You needn't worry, Sir, no one will get through the front door, not even you, I can assure you of that."

"No, Lurch, you can let me in, but no one else."

Lurch looked at the paper and read it through. "Sorry, Sir, I have explicit instructions to let no one in."

Butler returned to the note, added a few words and held it up so Lurch could read it. "What does it say now?"

"Absolutely under no circumstances let anyone through the door EXCEPT FOR BUTLER. Couldn't be plainer, Sir, you should have written that before and then there would not have been the recent misunderstanding."

"Yes, Lurch, as usual it's entirely my fault." For the fourth time Butler tried to leave the room.

"What about Ebenezer's special guest, Mrs. Muffins? Ebenezer loves her apple pies she bakes especially for him with extra cinnamon and a sugar plum in the middle. I'm sure he wouldn't mind her coming in, seeing how happy he always is after her visits."

"Gaaahhh! NO LURCH. NO ONE EXCEPT ME IS TO COME THROUGH THE DOOR UNTIL I RETURN!"

"There is no need to shout, Sir, my hearing is excellent."

Butler turned to leave but paused with his foot mid-step.

"What if someone comes through the window, Sir, is that okay?"

Butler's frustrated scream echoed through the house. He slammed the front door on his way out.

Lurch stared at the door. "Sir...?"

Furtive peered through the metal bars of the gate barring his way at the eight men on the other side staring back at him. His hand reached out to test the gate's strength. It was as solid as it looked. He gazed up at the slit in the ceiling the portcullis had dropped from. "Now, that's a surprise."

"Mr. Drooge said it might be," commented Flint, the man nearest the gate. "Okay, men, attack position!"

A flurry of activity ended with the guards in various positions of defence. The two at the front lay on the ground, the two behind knelt, the two behind crouched and the two at the back stood until every weapon they held had a clear shot at Furtive.

"Impressive," Furtive praised.

Flint beamed with delight from Furtive's praise. "Load weapons!"

A series of metallic clacks spread down the corridor until a grinding crunch of metal and a curse spoilt the effect.

"What a piece of crap, it's jammed again."

Flint sighed and turned his head. "Perhaps, Figgins, if you cleaned it occasionally it would function as it's supposed to."

"Yeah, my fault that's what it is. Has anyone got some oil?"

"Rub it on Jekyll's head, his hair is greasier than one of Molly's fried breakfasts," joked Maggot.

"Oy, don't bring me into this," moaned Jekyll. "My gun is working fine."

"What's that stench, there's a right smelly stink coming from somewhere," said one of the men near the front.

"I think someone's trod in something," said another.

"I have some oil, Figgins," called out Furtive. "Pass it forward."

The jammed weapon started on its journey along the corridor.

"Sorry about this, Mr. Murdersin," Flint apologized. "There's always one rotten apple to spoil the barrel!"

"Oy, I can hear yer, you know," called out Figgins.

"Think nothing of it...Flint, isn't it?" enquired Furtive.

"That's correct, Sir. Flint Stone." He reached out a hand, causing Furtive to bend to grasp it as the man still laid on the floor. "It's an honour to make your acquaintance again, Mr. Murdersin."

When the weapon was passed through the bars, Furtive fished in a pocket and, after a brief scramble, pulled out a small flask of gun oil and began lubricating the pistol's moving parts. "That was an impressive move your men did just now, Flint, did you train them?"

"Thank you for the compliment, Sir, but though I do keep them in shape, I cannot take the praise for their training, that was done by another, Major Moriarty Holmes.

Furtive raised his eyebrows in surprise, halted his administrations upon the pistol's metal parts and looked at Flint. "That is even more impressive. Moriarty is said to be the best in the business."

"That he is, Sir, that he is. Mr. Sebastian spared no expense."

"Yes, something that is becoming very clear," Furtive mumbled. He pulled a rag from a pocket and attended to the inner workings of the weapon. "I overheard a story about Major Moriarty some time ago...?"

"...You did, Sir, I don't suppose you'd mind sharing it with me and the lads. It's a boring job this and it would really brighten up our evening."

Furtive glanced at the expectant faces and shrugged. "I'd be happy to, but tell me, before I start, does Moriarty have a small nick out of his right ear lobe?"

Flint nodded enthusiastically. "That he does, Sir."

"Good, that adds credence that the tale is true. I believe it took place about ten years ago. Major Moriarty was on a mission in the Peruvian jungle to seek out an ancient artefact said to give the one who possessed it a great power."

"What sort of power?" asked Flint.

"Please, no interruptions."

"Sorry, Sir, it won't happen again."

"Moriarty spent three months tracking down the lost city of Hellicum, an ancient Aztec city long abandoned by its people. Though overgrown with vegetation, trees and creepers, its details were vaguely discernible beneath the foliage. Using a machete to hack a path to its centre, Moriarty arrived at the building he sought, the Demon Temple of the Aztec priest, Skelemordor. He climbed the hundreds of steep steps that were slick with moisture and rotting vegetation leading up the face of the stone pyramid; a misplaced foot would have sent him hurtling to the ground and his death. After a laborious climb he reached the top. Slightly out of breath, Moriarty paused to survey the pyramid's peak. An altar, still stained from the thousands of human sacrifices Skelemordor had long ago presented to the Aztec's evil, blood-thirsty demon gods, held no interest to the first human to set eyes upon its macabre details for hundreds of years. It was the dark entrance of the small building set in the middle of the flat peak he headed for. Inside he found nothing; it was as empty as a hermit's address book.

"But Moriarty hadn't travelled all that way to be discouraged so easily. He examined every nook, cranny and stone until he finally discovered that which he sought; a loose stone. He pressed it. A slab in the middle of the floor dropped down and slid to one side. The lantern he lit and shone into the dark void picked out a stone staircase leading into the depths of the pyramid. Having no fear of what lay below, Moriarty descended. He searched every room on his way down, but found no sign of the precious object he was so desperate to unearth. Deeper and deeper he went, far deeper than the height of the pyramid he had climbed before, so deep he thought he would soon arrive in Hell itself. But still no fear did the man experience. His mind was set on one goal and he would not give up until the task became pointless or death prevented him from carrying on.

"After what seemed to be many hours, he finally arrived at the bottom. His only route to travel was an ominous dark tunnel cloaked in an atmosphere that warned one not to enter. Moriarty entered. It was the first time since he was a child that he experienced an inkling of fear. He sensed what lay at the tunnel's end was something beyond his imagination. The thought of the great prize spurred his legs forward and his concerns aside. And then he saw it..." Furtive paused and cocked the gun. Its mechanism functioned with a barely a whisper of oiled metal parts sliding across each other. He handed it through the bars and it was passed to Figgins at the back, who cocked it appreciatively as soon as it was in his grasp.

"Wow, that's great. Thanks, Mr. Murdersin."

"You are welcome, Figgins," said Furtive. "Now back to the story. Moriarty reached the end of the tunnel and stood at the entrance to a large cavern. His prize, the mysterious ancient artefact, waited tantalizingly for him upon a stone pedestal on the far side of the chamber. But Moriarty was no fool, he suspected the room was booby-trapped and as soon as he set one foot on the innocent looking floor all hell would break loose. For a few moments he stood there completing the dilemma he faced; how was he going to reach the artefact without setting off the traps? He concluded the mechanism for setting off the traps would be located within the smooth area of stone slabs that covered most of the floor; however, around the edge was a small area of rough floor no wider than his hand. It was this that would allow him safe passage to the pedestal. He would grab the artefact and retrace his steps around the edge back to the passage, along the tunnel, up the steps, down the side of the pyramid and head home through the jungle.

"Sound plan as it seemed, it did not work out as he envisaged. What Moriarty was unaware of, but was about to be, was that the Aztec engineer who had safeguarded the room was much sneakier than Moriarty had given him credit for. You see, the stone his size eleven boots currently stood on, had already primed the sequence of traps he was about to face.

"Confident with his plan, Moriarty kept his back to the wall and stepped onto the small ledge of rough stone running around the edge. As soon as his feet had left the stone block at the entrance, a loud grinding sound filled the cavern. Now, as I mentioned earlier, the man was no fool, he realized the consequences of the sound and that something very bad was about to happen. His eyes flicked between the passage and the ancient artefact he had no wish to leave behind. Throwing caution to the wind, he raced across the chamber and grabbed the artefact. As he turned to rush back to the passage, the grinding of stone seemed to judder before grinding to a stop. Moriarty smiled, the ancient mechanism had not survived the test of time; it had jammed, and he was perfectly safe.

"Keen to test the mysterious power of the artefact, he held it in both hands and stared into the ruby eyes of the grotesque god statue. The eyes began to glow. The statue became warm. Moriarty's body tingled from head to foot, his hair and moustache stood on end and then, without any warning a great..." Furtive stopped talking.

"Please Mr. Murdersin, don't stop," pleaded Jekyll, "*A great*, what?"

Furtive shrugged. "Sorry lads, I have no idea. I was robbing this gentleman's club at the time, one of those posh ones in London, and had been eavesdropping on the conservation in the clubroom next to the office where I was currently emptying the vault of all its valuables. So engrossed was I in the story, I failed to hear the man who stood in the open door staring at me, enter. I, of course, leapt out of the window before he could apprehend me. The result is I never heard the end of the story, but Moriarty obviously survived because you lot trained with him."

"But, with all due respect, Mr. Murdersin," said Flint. "Why start a story you don't know the end of?"

"It ain't fair," complained Maggot.

"Nevertheless, even without the ending it's still a damn good story." Furtive told them. "Kept you lot entertained for a few minutes."

"Yes, but there was *no* ending," admonished Flint. "It's just not done, Sir. It's so frustrating and we are going to spend ages trying to work out what that *great* thing was?"

"Perhaps it will help relieve the boredom you moaned about earlier."

"And what about the nick in Major Moriarty's right ear lobe, that weren't even mentioned," said Jekyll.

"Sorry, I forgot that bit," said Furtive. "Hanging from that earlobe used to be an earring in the shape of a tiny skull with two rubies set in its eye sockets; it looked really evil by all accounts. Anyway, as he was hacking his way through the Peruvian jungle, he was chased by a band of hungry cannibals who were keen on making Moriarty their next meal. His only way to escape was to jump off this cliff into the raging river below. When he leapt off the edge, the earring got caught on a twig and was ripped off, taking with it a bit of his ear lobe. It is said, even to this day, those cannibals still worship that earring as their god."

"I thought it was gonna be something more exciting than that?" moaned Jekyll.

"What a bloody let down," complained another.

Sensing he was losing his audience's interest, Furtive said, "Now open this gate and let me through."

"Sorry, Sir, that is beyond my means," said Flint. "Mr. Sabastian has the only key."

"Furtive glanced at the lock. No matter, I'll soon pick it and have it open."

"Sorry, Sir, you step one foot this side of that barrier and it might be the only part of you recognizable after we have all fired our weapons."

Furtive could tell by the man's stern gaze, however much the man feared Murdersin, he wasn't going to disobey his employer's strict orders. Furtive smiled. "Well done, Flint. Sebastian said you were a good man and now I know that to be true."

Flint let out a relieved sigh. "Thank you very much, Sir. Mr. Drooge said you might come and check on security."

He is an astute man, your employer."

"He is that, Sir. So...did we pass your test?"

Furtive noticed every face in the corridor looked at him expectantly. "Of course you have all passed, cut my legs off and call me Shorty if you didn't. A finer bunch of men have never been caught in my gaze than those standing before me now."

The men cheered and congratulated themselves. One man, yes him at the back again, forgetting where he was, fired his pistol in celebration. The bullet ricocheting around the passage caused everyone to dive to the floor. It struck a metal bar of the gate above Flint's head and pinged through the open door.

The men glanced at behind at Figgins and the smoke curling from his pistol.

He grinned. "Works fine now, Mr. Murdersin." Figgins peered through the bars of the gate at the far end of the corridor. "Mr. Murdersin?"

11th CHAPTER

DIABLO

The hunchback in the quarry was worried. He had a strong feeling he was being watched. The evil red eyes peering at him from the darkness did nothing to belay the feeling. But however hard he strained his ears, he heard no sounds of anyone following. He stared at the red eyes again. He knew there were no dangerous animals in Britain, so it had to be some harmless creature, a badger, a fox, maybe a weasel or a stoat, but probably a pet cat turned feral. "Here, kitty, kitty. It's okay, I won't hurt you."

Diablo's thoughts were not as comforting. If the human took one step closer it would abandon its previous plan, leap upon the man's meaty carcass and rip it to shreds before feeding on the flesh. It would be a pleasant change from the tough old mutton it was fed every day. Oh, how it hated mutton. Well aware its creaking bones and tired muscles would not perform as they once did, it had slipped past the human so it could attack from the front. Then, if its dinner fled, it would head deeper into the quarry and away from the only possible exit. It crouched behind the rock when the human began to move again, when both expectant diner and unaware dinner were distracted. Both turned their gaze toward the sound.

The hunchback, as curious as a cat with only one life left and that was hanging on a very strained thread, approached the wall of rock where the sound came from and cocked an ear. His eyes travelled up the cliff and focused on the small dark opening where the sounds of scuffling and cursing drifted out.

Remaining at his slightly higher advantage point, Diablo traversed along the small ledge of rock and stared across the clearing at the strange, but tasty, looking fat-backed human and followed its gaze to the hole in the rock.

It was difficult to say who of the three were more surprised at the sudden unexpected meeting; Furtive, the hunchback or Diablo perched on the rock with jaws agape.

Furtive recovered quickly from the surprise, smiled at the hunchback below and said, "Fancy meeting you here."

The hunchback's mouth opened but no words came out.

Diablo caressed its yellow teeth with its tongue. It seemed he was going to have double helpings tonight.

Furtive had not hung about to see the bullet pass through the space he had vacated a split second before its arrival. As soon as he had realized there would be no escape through the guard-filled corridor, even if he'd had in his possession his namesake's legendary fruit knife, he had rushed back to Sebastian's private museum to see if his only alternative route of escape was possible.

He pulled the logs from the fire grate, stuck his head in the fireplace and with a candle held high to light up the flue, he gazed up the chimney. He was not filled with hope and happiness by what he saw, but there was a slim chance he could make it if he got rid of the hump. He slipped off the coat with the attached padded hump the painting was concealed within. Stretched the aches from a back not used to being bent over at such an angle for a pronged amount of time, plunged a hand into a pocket and grabbed the item he sought. One end of the ball of string he pulled out was tied around the coat collar and the other end attached to his belt. He grabbed the whisky decanter and took a long gulp, stuffed a handful of cigars in a pocket that seemed to be of infinite proportions, fished out his head lamp, lit in, slipped the ring over his head and he was ready.

He slithered into the narrow confines of the chimney and began his climb. Though soot covered the sides, it was not of an abundance to indicate the fire was lit very often. Furtive grunted, groaned and cursed as he pulled, clawed, pushed and shoved his protesting body up the claustrophobic tube. When he arrived at the top ten minutes later, he let his sweaty soot streaked face bathe in the breeze from an opening a short distance away. He dragged his body out of the chimney, crawled through the short tunnel and poked his head out into the cool night air. Sensing he was not alone, he directed his gaze from the heavens to the earth. His eyes did a double take. His eyebrows rose to peer over the large false nose blocking their view. His fear thermometer began to bubble. His lips formed words as casually as they could in the circumstances and addressed the hunchback he was impersonating. "Fancy meeting you here." The reply he received a few moments later, though only one simple word, could not have confused him more if it was spoken in Russian.

The hunchback looked up at the face that matched his own. "Crakett?"

Furtive stared at his mirror image. The name that had just been uttered had undeniably been posed as a question. There could only be one reason, the hunchback below was also not the real Crakett Murdersin. "Wait, there, I'll be down in a minute."

Furtive returned to the chimney opening, untied the string from his belt and pulled up the hump padded coat. Though difficult and grazing-elbows awkward to slip the unwieldy padded coat on in the small tunnel, the task was soon completed. Furtive slipped over the edge and scrambled none to gracefully down the rock.

Diablo had used the distraction to slip farther along the quarry and had selected a suitable ambush point. Though killing both strange humans would not be easy, or probably pain free for its old limbs, it was confident it could carry out the double slaying. If the attacked proved successful it wouldn't have to eat mutton for a week or more. It was a very pleasing thought. It slunk into the shadows and waited.

"I don't understand why you are here, Mr. Murdersin. I thought you were going to Drooge Manor."

Furtive assumed the hunchback imposter who had disappeared from the carriage and now stood before him, was a decoy arranged by the real Murdersin. Perhaps this hunchback was also a thief and set to the task he had just carried out. Furtive's quick thinking came into play. "When you failed to show up at the castle I had to initiate a backup plan and carry out your job as well."

"Sorry about that, Mr. Murdersin, but it wasn't my fault. I fell out of the coach and ended up down here in the quarry."

Furtive shrugged his hump. "These things happen, which is why I always have a backup plan."

"Very wise, Sir." The hunchback glanced at his shoes and wiped the souls on the ground. "I think I may have trodden in something." He then tilted his head from side to side as he examined his twin.

"Is something wrong?" Furtive asked.

"Oh, no, nothing wrong Mr. Murdersin, you just seem a bit different from when I saw you last, but it was rather dark when we met."

"That would explain it."

"Yes, Sir, but the dark wouldn't explain your voice, which sounds nothing like it did previously, or that you are now a few inches taller, would it?"

"I suppose not, but what would, was if the voice you heard before was not my real voice. I have many I call upon to keep my identity a secret if the need arises. As to my height, I often change it to make me less identifiable. Is this better?" Furtive forced his protesting spine to bend a little more.

"Well that explains it then, Sir, though I fail to comprehend how altering your height slightly or disguising your voice would prevent anybody from recognizing you from your unique face, bent over posture and the rather large hump on your back. But that is your concern."

"It most certainly is," said Furtive, gruffly.

"Is the voice you are using now your real voice?"

Furtive shrugged. "Perhaps, perhaps not, but I do a really good impression of a pirate if you want to hear it?"

"Not really, I'd rather know what happens now, and will I still get paid?"

"That is something I will dwell on. As to your former enquiry, it may seem a strange request, but I have my reasons and it's important you answer with as much detail as you can recall. What did I tell you I was going to do tonight while you were in Drooge Castle?"

"Well, Sir, you didn't say a lot about that at all. You just told me you had to go to Drooge Manor and I had to go to the castle, pretend to be you and do what Sebastian Drooge requested of me."

"I said nothing about stealing any paintings?"

The hunchback shook his head. "Not a whisper. I guess you are not the sort to share more than you have to."

"Exactly." Furtive glanced around the quarry. "I have much to do, so let's get out of here."

The hunchback pointed to the right. "That way, Sir. The other's a dead end, as I found out earlier."

"Okay, lead on."

The hunchback led, and the other hunchback followed.

Diablo watched its double helping of dinner come nearer and nearer and nearer. When they were the other side of the rock it crouched behind, it jumped on top and leapt into the air. Something cracked; it was its damn spine again. It felt like red hot pokers were jabbing mercilessly at his backbone. Diablo twisted in agony in mid-air and thumped to the ground.

Furtive froze. "What was that?"

"What, I didn't hear anything," the hunchback replied.

Diablo dragged its aching body into the shadows, every movement a fresh source of pain.

Furtive turned and scanned the area. They glimpsed nothing but dirt, rock and darkness.

"Probably the cat I saw earlier," suggested the hunchback.

Furtive ended his search and carried on along the quarry.

Around the next bend the castle loomed high above them. It had been built almost level with the edge of the quarry's rocky side. Though most of its windows were dark, a couple shone with candlelight.

They stepped into the shadows when a window in the castle above opened and something was thrown out. It landed at their feet with a soft unappetizing thump. They both looked at the haunch of stringy mutton.

"Now, who or what do you think that's for?" said Furtive.

"Probably for that cat," said the hunchback., naively.

Furtive looked at the large piece of meat, doubtfully. "If that's for a cat, it's not the cute and cuddly one you're picturing in your mind. Come on, let's go."

The hunchback cast a nervous glance back into the quarry and quickly checked his shoes again before following.

Diablo watched its human dinner walk away, smelt the unappetizing aroma of the tough chunk of meat and reluctantly dragged its painful body towards it. *Damn, mutton again.*

At the end of the quarry a high stone block wall blocked their way.

"I wonder why that's there," said the hunchback.

"I have no idea, but I suspect it's to keep something in rather than anything out." Furtive picked out a metal framework in the darkness where the wall met natural rock and walked over. "It's a lift of some kind." He turned to the hunchback. "Can you climb these metal supports?"

The hunchback looked doubtfully at the tall metal struts interspersed with cross beams. "In or out of this costume, it's unlikely."

The Lost Inheritance Mystery

Furtive pointed out a metal cage level with the top of the wall. "I'll climb up and lower that down to you."

"Thank you, Mr. Murdersin, and I must say your vicious reputation is not deserved."

"I think your opinion will change when you encounter the real me." Furtive gripped one of the metal supports and shimmied up it like it was a rope. He reached the top in no time and released the ratchet that sent the cage to the ground. When the hunchback had climbed aboard, he turned the wheel the cage chain was connected to and hoisted him up.

"Well, what now," asked the hunchback when he was back on solid ground.

Furtive gazed at the distant building and pointed. "We go to Drooge Manor."

The two hunchbacks walked off along the track that took them away from Castle Drooge.

Buckley was confused, not an astounding declaration I admit, but nevertheless confused was what he was. His instructions were clear in his mind: if he saw someone who looked like Mr. Murdersin, he was to fire the pistol he now held in preparation of doing just that. But should he? Because it would be impossible for three hunchbacks to look so alike, it was obvious to him that Mr. Murdersin, the man who had given him the order, must be one of the identical hunchbacks walking along the road toward his

- 148 -

position. He decided to wait until they were closer before making his decision.

So indecisive was Buckley that even when they were almost level with him he still had no idea what he should do. To hopefully find out, he stepped out from his hiding place to talk to them. "Sorry to interrupt your evening stroll, Mr. Murdersin..." His eyes flicked hopefully from one hunchback to the other.

Furtive relieved the man's tension. "Yes, what is it?"

"Oh, good, it is you, Mr. Murdersin, though you seem a little taller and your voice sounds a little different, not so deep and menacing."

"It's not his real voice, but he does a good pirate impression, apparently," said the hunchback.

"You do, Sir. I'd like ter hear that. I can do some bird calls. They ain't very good but..."

"Quiet, both of you." Furtive stared at Buckley sternly. "Clearly it's me, who else would it be?"

"Well, ignoring the person beside you who looks identical, no one, Sir. It's just that your instructions were to fire my pistol," he waved it in the air for emphasis, "if I saw anyone that looked like you coming along this very road, but when I spied the two of you I thought there's no point in firing my pistol to let you know he was coming when you are already with the one I was to warn you about." He took a deep breath. He felt a headache fast approaching.

"You are correct, of course there is no need to fire your pistol when I am already here."

Buckley was very relieved. "Did I do good, Mr. Murdersin?"

"Good might be pushing it. However, for your next task, I want you to round up all the men watching the manor and have them spread out around the castle. There's an attack pending, and Sebastian wants every man available protecting his property from intruders."

Buckley stood up straight and saluted. "Yes, Sir, you can count on me again, Sir."

"I knew I could. Now be off with you. Round the men up as quickly as you can."

Buckley hurried off into the darkness.

"Shouldn't we get inside the castle before the attack starts?" asked the hunchback, anxiously.

"No need, I lied."

"You did! But why do you want Sebastian's men away from the manor? Are they not on our side?"

"I suppose that depends on what side we are on. Remain quiet and follow me."

Furtive led the slightly confused hunchback toward the large house.

Butler had just finished his check of the grounds and knocked on the front door.

"Who is it?" Lurch asked. "Unless your name is..." There was a rustle of paper. "...Butler, I can't let you in. Is your name Butler?"

Butler sighed. "Yes, my name is Butler."

"Then please enter, the door is unlocked."

Butler entered and locked and bolted the door. "It's probably not a good idea to mention you will only let someone in with the name of Butler and then ask them if that is their name."

"It's not, Sir? Then how am I to know who is wanting to come in?"

"Just ask them their name."

"But that's what I did, Sir. I asked you if your name was Butler, and it was, and you are, so it worked."

Butler gave up. "I did a walk around, but apart from Sebastian's idiots littering the grounds everything is quiet, too quiet."

"Would you like me to fetch my drum kit and make some noise, Mr. Butler?"

"No, thank you, Lurch. I'll endure the silence."

"As you wish, Sir, but let me know if you change your mind."

"I will, but it's unlikely."

TRING! TRING!

"It's the front door bell, Sir."

"Thank you for reminding me. Now go and do the same as you did last time."

"Eh, last time, Sir?"

"Open the door to find out who it is, but don't let them in unless I say."

"Unless you say *what*, Sir?"

"Unless I tell you to let them in."

"Okay, Sir, I have it now." Lurch headed into the hall and crossed to the front door. He slid back the bolts, turned the key in the lock and swung the door open. He looked at the two men standing on the step and turned his head to look back at Butler. "I think we may have a problem, Sir."

Butler peered around the door frame and saw the two Crakett Murdersin's.

One of them waved. "Hi, Butler." His hand then indicated the man beside them. "Don't look so worried, this is another imposter and not the real Crakett Murdersin."

Butler stepped into the hall and aimed his blunderbuss pistol at the two hunchbacks. "Let them in Lurch and lock the door. You two come into the study."

Presently engaged in searching for the hiding place of Ebenezer's painting, Shadow was unaware of the events taking place on the floor above. The search had started in the attic and worked its way down. After all other rooms in the house had been discounted as a possible hiding place, Shadow's thorough investigation currently concentrated on the wine cellar. If it was not here it wasn't in the house and the outbuildings would be next to suffer the assassin-thief's searching gaze.

Shadow strolled down each rack of dusty wine bottles and was impressed by some of the rare vintages. It was in the last rack the clue being searched for was found; something not quite right. In this instance it was a wine bottle with finger marks disturbing its dusty covering. Shadow pulled it from its spot and glanced at the label to find it a rather uninspiring wine of a doubtful vintage. A gaze into the empty slot revealed something much more rewarding, an iron handle in the wall. A black gloved hand reached in and pulled.

CLICK!

The middle section of the wine rack sprung proud.

Shadow replaced the bottle in its niche, pulled the secret door open and stepped inside.

Crakett Murdersin, also unaware of his two lookalikes inside the house, slipped through the round roof window, followed Furtive's tracks in the dust covered beams and dropped silently to the floor. He passed through the door and traversed the narrow staircase. The tripwires and carpet traps removed by Butler were no longer a hindrance. He paused at the top of the grand staircase and cocked an ear. His keen hearing picked up muffled voices and identified the room they came from. He slid down the banister and landed softly in the hall. After a quick search of the ground floor he found the door leading to the cellar. His climb down the stairs created not a sound. His walk to the far end of the wine cellar produced no clue to the hiding place of Ebenezer's painting. He had better luck on spying the open secret door in the end wall. He paused for a few moments to contemplate the obvious evidence he was not the only one looking and they were at this moment closer to finding it. With caution guiding his way, he slipped through the door.

Ben Hammott

AN UNEXPECTED GATHERING

Butler, though pleased with Furtive's successful acquisition of Sebastian's painting, was still coming to terms with the unexpected appearance of two Crakett Murdersin's. He had also just been informed by Furtive that the real Crakett Murdersin, if he wasn't already in the house, probably planned on doing that very thing. It explained the reason why he would use an imposter to take his place while he robbed the manor.

"And it gets worst, Butler," said Furtive. "Sebastian has also hired another to steal the painting, one who goes by the name of *Shaaadoooow*, and I said the name all mysterious to try and convey the menace this accomplished thief and assassin poses. I do know a story about the Shadow if you want to hear it?"

"That won't be necessary as I expect it lacks the required ending." Butler turned to the other fake hunchback in the room. "Who are you?"

"No one really, I'm a theatre actor. Arthur Milkwood is my name. Perhaps you have heard of me?" he asked hopefully.

Butler shook his head. "I don't often get the chance for pleasurable activities, though after your disastrous performance so far tonight I doubt viewing any play Arthur Milkwood starred in could be described as pleasurable. But I digress. To get everything straight in my mind, you, Arthur, were in the carriage?"

He nodded. "Until I fell out and rolled into the quarry."

"The real Crakett Murdersin hired you to impersonate him so he could come here and steal the painting."

Arthur shrugged. "He failed to inform me of his plans, just that he wanted me to impersonate him. I only accepted because I was between parts, and have been for some time, and in desperate need of the money he offered, which I still hope to receive."

Butler thought aloud. "A possible scenario is the real Crakett found out that Sebastian hired Shadow to steal the painting and jealous rivalry led him to substitute you for him to go to the castle, while he came here to steal the painting before Shadow."

"That probably means Crakett, and possibly Shadow, are already in the house," said Furtive.

"I agree," said Butler. "We must go and protect the painting. If it's stolen, none of us will get paid." He turned to the Milkwood. "Except perhaps for you, although so far you haven't done anything to earn it." Butler aimed the pistol that had rested in his lap at the actor. "Unless of course, *you* are the real Crakett and everything you have done up to this point has been a clever plan to gain entry into this house."

"Now hang on a minute, I am no more the real Crakett than the foul breath one sitting next to me."

Butler wasn't convinced. "Prove it, remove your disguise."

The hurting end of the pistol pointed at him persuaded Milkwood he best do as instructed. He removed the padded coat, wig and mask. "Now do you believe me?"

"Okay, so you are not Crakett, but I still don't trust you. You could still be part of his plan to steal the painting. Lurch, fetch the rope from the kitchen and tie him up."

Lurch went to do Butler's bidding.

"Is that really necessary?" asked Milkwood.

"It is. You'll be set free in the morning, or when all this is over."

Furtive stood. "I don't suppose I'll be needing this disguise anymore?"

"No, take it off; it's too confusing when there is more than one Crakett around. As soon as Milkwood's secured, we'll head downstairs to collect Ebenezer's painting."

Furtive stripped off his disguise, donned his own coat and placed his crumpled top hat on his head. "Furtive is back!"

Butler smiled. "You did well tonight. I know your part in this should end now, but I'd appreciate it if you helped me sort things out here. I'll make sure you get paid for the extra work."

"I would have stayed even without the offer of payment, Butler, not that I'm gonna refuse it mind yer, but I like you lot, so if yer needs me help, yer've got it."

Butter nodded. "Thanks."

Lurch returned with the rope and Furtive, an expert in all types of knots, tied him securely to the chair. Butler ordered Lurch to stand in the doorway, so he could guard the prisoner and at the same time keep an eye on the hallway; he then led Furtive down to the wine cellar where they discovered signs of an intruder.

The two men stared at the open secret door.

"At least one of them has found it," said Furtive.

Worry creased Butler's brow. "Let's hope we are not too late and they haven't already absconded with the painting."

They lit the lanterns they had brought with them and passed through the door.

With slow cautious movements, they descended the stone steps arched with natural rock, their ears staining to hear the tell-tale signs of an intruder below. They heard nothing but intermittent drips of water. They paused at the bottom and cast their gaze around the large cavern mostly taken up with a pool of crystal clear water. Drops of water dripped from some of the stalactites formed over the centuries to splash in the pool and send out ripples. A rickety wooden bridge snaked between stalagmites protruding from the water. Some had met their opposites to form large, pale, glistening columns of hard mineral.

"It looks like a fairy grotto," whispered Furtive in amazement.

"Whoever's down here has crossed the bridge," said Butler, worried by the lack of cover the wooden walkway would offer when they crossed.

Furtive peered into the shadows cloaking most of the bridge and the darkness beyond. Though he saw no signs of movement, someone could be hiding and watching them. "Where does it lead?"

"To a tunnel that leads to another chamber and then to Ebenezer's secret study."

"We could just wait here until whoever's down here returns."

"We could, but there's a secret escape route. If someone is down here who has your uncanny sense of detection, they might find it and escape that way. We'll have to carry on." Butler approached the pool and stepped onto the bridge. It creaked and swayed with each step, however carefully he moved. He chose haste and rushed across with Furtive close on his heels. They reached the far side of the pool and entered the dark tunnel. Butler slowed at a bend and peered around the corner. He saw nothing in the darkness. Whoever was down here would need light to move about; he took the lack of one to mean the tunnel was safe. He continued along it.

The next chamber they entered was small and contained a few old, mildewed half rotten wooden packing cases. They headed for the exit on the far side, but Butler halted so abruptly Furtive bumped into him.

Butler turned to face him and quickly stepped back to a safer distance. "I just saw a flash of light, take my lamp and wait here while I look."

Furtive took the lantern and watched Butler creep towards the opening and peer around the rock.

Shadow, watched them both.

Crakett, unaware of the eyes upon him, stood in the middle of the furnished chamber. He held up a lantern to spread its light as wide as possible and looked for any place where the painting might be hidden. The room smelt of long disuse and decay. Though the armchair, small table, desk and chair and bookcases must have once looked luxurious, time and damp air had turned them into objects of faded splendour. The once fine collection of books on the now sagging shelves, were little more than worm eaten mildewed pages and food for the mushrooms sprouting from their bindings.

Butler returned to Furtive and whispered. "It's Crakett. He's looking for the painting."

"What do we do?"

Butler shrugged. "I've no idea, but if he gets hold of the painting it will ruin Ebenezer. It's his only hope of a future, and mine. We have to stop him."

"I don't understand. If Sebastian and Ebenezer split the inheritance when their father died, why is Ebenezer so worse off. Look at that place of his upstairs, its falling apart."

"Sebastian tricked Ebenezer when they divided up the businesses. Ebenezer ended up with so many debts it almost ruined him."

"I thought there weren't something right about the man when I met him. He said the family treasure was nothing but a trinket, a family heirloom of no value."

"He was lying. When the castle was under construction the workers in the quarry Jacobus owned, stumbled across a rich gold seam in the rock; you can still see the old mine workings today. The rumours are he mined a huge quantity of gold by the time it petered out and he kept most of it, but where it is today no one knows."

Furtive's eyes lit up. "And that's what yer think the clues in the painting will lead too?"

"I'm certain of it. But if Sebastian gets there first no one else will see a flake of it."

"It will be a shame to lose Ebenezer's painting now we have Sebastian's in our possession and so close to finding out where this treasure is."

"That's why we have to prevent Crakett from finding it."

"And how do we do that?"

"I think, Furtive, it is time to put your considerable skills to the test again. I did consider you creeping up on him and knocking him out with something, but I'm worried he might smell you if you get too close."

"Fair point," Furtive agreed. He tapped his jacket. "I do have Grave Filler I could use."

"After hearing that half-story you told me about him fighting off thirty armed men, I'm not sure that would work. We need stealth and cunning if we are going to succeed. I want you to creep inside and distract him long enough for me to come up from behind and whack him on the head."

"Not even as remotely cunning as yer previous plan, but it could work. My part will not be a problem. He will be so distracted a marching band could creep up on him." Furtive placed the lanterns on the ground and crept over to the opening.

Butler blinked, and the man was gone. He moved over to the wall and peered around the edge. As soon as Furtive's distraction began he would make his move.

Shadow pondered what had just been overheard. What had started out as a simple job had suddenly grown very complicated; Shadow did not like complications. It explained the hunchback's presence, but Crakett was wasting his time, Shadow had already searched the mouldy study and the painting wasn't there. This talk of paintings leading to gold was though, an intriguing development worth considering. Sebastian was not a man to be trusted and doubts had already been festering as whether it was wise to continue with the original assignment. The inheritance just mentioned could provide a much richer reward. Shadow decided to remain a little longer to see what else revealed itself.

Crakett set about spilling the books onto the ground and pulling the decrepit book shelves from the walls in his search for a hidden storage space or chamber. The first bookcase crashed to the ground in a heap of mouldy books and rotten wood. He gripped the second, twitched his nose and checked the soles of his shoes.

"I'm quite certain Ebenezer would disapprove of yer methods," said Furtive. "Yes, the bookshelves have suffered a certain amount of neglect, but nevertheless they still belong ter him."

As Crakett spun his hand dived beneath his coat, pulled out a pistol and aimed it at the man reclining in the mildewed armchair whilst puffing on a cigar. "Who in hell's name are you?"

"My name, Sir, is *Shadow*!" Furtive lied.

"The Shadow!" There was a certain amount of nervousness in Crakett's surprised reply, evidence he was aware of the assassin-thief's reputation.

"Unlike you, the one and only and no need to be formal, you can drop the *the*."

"What are you doing here?"

"The very question I was about to ask you. I'm not sure Sebastian will be very pleased when he discovers you sent an incompetent imposter to guard his precious painting while you came here to steal Ebenezer's."

Though a little surprised the man was so well informed, Crakett had a suspicion he was not all he claimed to be. "If you really are Shadow, why am I still alive? Your reputation would have my bloody corpse spread atop that pile of mouldy books by now."

"Oh, I must apologize. Did you want to die so quickly? If you do it would take but a moment to satisfy your desire." He casually puffed on the cigar and blew a long stream of smoke at Crakett.

Crakett's hump heaved when he coughed and choked on the pungent smoke tainted with Furtive's breath. A little green and in a hoarse voice, he uttered, "If that foul stench is produced by the quality of that cigar, I suggest you change your brand."

"The cigar is fine, one of Sebastian's actually. He offered me one, I took many, but ter return to your query of why you still draw breath, even if it is not as fresh as yer would like. It is because I am curious to discover why yer would go ter so much trouble ter substitute your persona for another, who, by the way, is currently bound to a chair in Ebenezer's study."

Crakett's raised eyebrows signalled his surprise.

"And also, why you decided, against Sebastian's orders, to come here and do the very job *I* was contracted to do? Something I am not over-thrilled about."

"The explanation is simple, greed! I learned of the brothers lost inheritance and how much it's rumoured to be worth, so I thought why have crumbs when you can have the whole cake."

"That you came here to steal Ebenezer's painting for yerself is something I can understand, if not forgive, but how will that help yer? Yer must know both paintings are required to find out where the treasure's hidden."

"I must admit, my current plan was not my first, but when I saw someone, who I now assume to be you, also disguised to look like me and swopped places with that damn fool of an actor in the carriage, I thought you must be a thief hired by Ebenezer to steal Sebastian's painting. This was good, as it left me free to concentrate on stealing Ebenezer's. I would then steal Sebastian's from you if you managed to steal it. Because you are here, I assume it is something you have already done."

Furtive nodded. "But you still don't know where either of the paintings are hidden?"

"You or Butler will have hidden Sebastian's upstairs somewhere," he glanced at the half-destroyed bookcases, "the other, I suspect, is in here somewhere. Soon both will be in my possession and the Drooge brothers' lost inheritance shortly after."

"I must say I am a little impressed, if very doubtful of your success."

"Okay, I'll play your little game a while longer. Why are you doubtful?"

There was a change in the hunchback that worried Furtive. He had suddenly grown more confident. "What game would that be?"

Without turning his gaze away from Furtive, Crakett thrust the arm holding the pistol to aim at Butler a few steps behind. "The game where your accomplice creeps up behind me and cracks me on the head, of course."

"Oh, that game," said Furtive.

Butler froze with the hand gripping the pistol by the barrel paused at the peak of its swing towards Crakett's head.

"I suggest, Butler, you drop your weapon before I am tempted to send a bullet speeding for your heart."

Butler's pistol clattered to the floor.

"You should have shot me while you had the chance," said Crakett.

"So that's where I went wrong. How silly of me. Would you mind if I had another go?"

Crakett motioned with the pistol. "Come and stand beside your friend."

"Friend is pushing it a bit. I hardly know the man."

"Thanks for that, Butler. Another name to cross off my Christmas card list."

Butler looked at him doubtfully.

"What's that look fer? You think I don't have any friends ter send cards ter? Well, you're wrong, as I have many."

Butler's doubt remained.

"There's Lurch for one, Ebenezer, for two. Arthur the actor. Yes, I tied him up, but he seems a forgiving kind of person. Now let me see, who else..."

"Shut up," ordered Crakett. "What in hell's name is wrong with you two? Don't you realize the situation you are in? God give me strength. I feel like putting a bullet in my brain just to put an end to this madness."

"Don't let us stop you," said Furtive.

"But if you do shoot your brains out, would it be possible to aim the pistol away from me?"

Butler stroked a hand over his sleeve. "You see, brains are so hard to remove from wool."

"Shut up both of you. You're giving me a headache."

"Maybe you should go upstairs and lie down for a while until it passes. We'll wait here, won't we Shadow?"

"As sure as beef is mutton," Furtive stated firmly.

Crakett took a deep breath to calm himself. "I believe you two are failing to recognize the advantage I have."

"What advantage would that be then?" Furtive asked.

Crakett waved the pistol in his face. "This advantage."

"Hmmm, yes, though it does seem that way, I'm quite convinced yer believe yer have more of an advantage than yer actually do. There be two of us and, if my observation is correct, as it normally is, the pistol yer hold steadily aimed at Butler's heart is the single shot model. As soon as yer pull the trigger I shall be upon yer before the bullet enters its victim's flesh and yer will be dead before Butler crashes to the ground."

"Um, let's not be too hasty with these morbid assumptions," argued Butler. "I'd prefer a scenario where my body did not end up on the ground, I mean, just look at it. It's damp and there's mould and mildew on everything. My clothes would be ruined."

"I think, with that particular scenario, Butler, damage to your clothes should not be the most drastic outcome you should be focusing on." Crakett turned to Furtive. "Now, whoever you are, because Shadow you certainly are not, or I would be dead, to answer your concern about two against one." A pistol, which he pulled from under his coat so swiftly it was almost impossible to notice the man's hand had moved, appeared in his other hand with it steadily pointed at Furtive.

Furtive stared down the barrel of the recently revealed menacing weapon. "Well, I am certainly glad we cleared that little matter up."

"I've had enough of all this time wasting. Butler, where has Ebenezer hidden his painting?"

"I'm sure I have no idea. I know it's down here somewhere, but I was never allowed to stay when Ebenezer removed it from its hiding place."

Crakett thrust the pistol in Butler's face. "I don't believe you."

"That may be, Crakett, but that doesn't automatically mean I am lying. Believe me, there is nothing more likely to persuade me to speak the absolute truth than that tarnished thing perched at the end of my nose. Don't you ever clean it?" Butler held out a hand. "Give it to me; I have some excellent ointment upstairs that will have it looking like new in no time."

Crakett narrowed his eyes as he glared at the two men. "You two are up to something." Keeping the weapons trained on his captives, Crakett shot a quick glance behind. Spying nothing to cause him concern he refocused his attention back on his captives. "You have ten seconds to tell me where the painting is, or I shoot your friend."

Butler glanced toward the entrance. "Has someone I like arrived?"

"He means me," said Furtive, sulkily.

Crakett began counting down. "Ten...nine..."

"Hey, hold on a minute, yer are counting too fast," Furtive said. "Yer should say, ten elephants...nine elephants, and so on, that's how yer count real seconds."

Crakett smirked. "eight...seven..."

"Sorry to interrupt your speed counting, Crakett," Butler apologized, "but is it alright if I took a step to the side. It's the blood spray I'm worried about. The wool suit you see."

"You so much as twitch and I'll put a large hole directly in the breast pocket of that damn precious suit of yours." He focused back on Furtive. "Now, where was I?"

"Nine, I believe," said Furtive, hopefully.

"Six...five..."

"It's very musty down here don't you think, Crakett? I'd like to go outside and *breathe* in the fresh air and let it out in a *long gasp* to clear the lungs."

Puzzled, Crakett and Furtive looked at Butler.

"You are going nowhere, Butler," Crakett told him.

Butler stared at Furtive. "Yes, a nice big *breath* of air is what is needed to clear the lungs of this *foul air.*"

"Stop talking!" ordered Crakett. "Four...three..."

When Furtive eventually realized what Butler was hinting at, he smiled. It wasn't very cunning, but it should be very effective.

"Two..."

Furtive drew in a lungful of air and let it out in a violent whoosh directed at Crakett's face.

"One!" Furtive's breath dived into Crakett's mouth and clawed its way up his nose. Crakett gagged. His eyes watered. His stomach heaved. His lips screamed.

Furtive knocked the gun aside as the hunchback squeezed the trigger. The bullet buried itself in the mouldy stuffing beside his head. The loud retort echoed around the chamber before fading to a whisper.

Butler wrenched the other weapon from Crakett's hand, turned it over, gripped the barrel, brought the butt down on Crakett's head and quickly moved away from the drifting cloud of vomit inducing breath.

Crakett's consciousness heaved a sigh of relief as his body slumped unconscious to the ground.

Shadow, who had observed proceedings from halfway across the room, encountered the dissipating tendrils of Crakett's foul breath. With hands firmly clamped over nose and mouth and the urge to gag and run screaming from the cavern suppressed, the thief assassin slunk to a safer distance.

"Great idea, that, Butler. I've never thought as using me smelly breath as a weapon before."

Butler, who had retreated a safe distance away, nodded. "Just promise when I am around, you'll only use it in a dire emergency."

"For you, Butler, anything. By the way, yer weren't serious were yer, when yer told Crakett we ain't friends?"

"As serious as you were about your Christmas card list."

Furtive tried to work out the meaning, but it was too much thinking. He gave up and accepted that Butler had been joking and playing for time. "What do we do now?"

"We grab the painting and get out of here before Shadow turns up."

"Oh, yeah, I forgot about that complication. Yer really do know where the painting is then?"

"I do, but first we need to do something about the hunchback." Butler thought for a few moments before deciding on a solution. "Do you have any rope in one of your bottomless pockets?"

"I'm a burglar, ain't I, of course I have rope." Furtive stuck a hand in a pocket. "Do yer have any preference to colour, thickness or weave?"

"I don't care as long as it's strong enough to keep Crakett secure. I'll send Lurch down to carry him up top."

When Crakett was tightly bound, Butler retrieved his pistol and headed for the exit.

Furtive was again confused. "I thought we were getting the painting?"

"We are. It's not in this room."

Furtive followed Butler.

Shadow, at a safe distance, followed Furtive.

Butler halted at the edge of the wide natural pool, knelt, plunged a hand into the cold water and after a quick search it reappeared gripping a chain. He pulled up the slack and hoisted out a thin metal cylinder.

Furtive was impressed. "Very sneaky, Butler. I never would have thought of looking in the water."

"We hoped no one would. When Sebastian's attempts to get his hands on the painting became more aggressive, I suggested to Ebenezer we move it from the other room as it was a too obvious a hiding place. I suggested the pool would be far better and less apparent. I had this watertight cylinder made and for the last two years this is where it has lain." Butler unscrewed one end of the sealed canister and tipped it up. Another slighter smaller metal container slid out. He dropped the larger tube on the floor and led Furtive up to the house.

With an impressed expression hidden beneath the black mask, Shadow paused to stare at the empty cylinder for a few moments. It was as Furtive said, a very sneaky hiding place and one that even Shadow would have overlooked. It was evidence that Butler was not a foe to be underestimated.

Butler and Furtive returned to the study. Lurch was sent to collect Crakett from the cavern and returned a few minutes later with the hunchback slung over one shoulder.

Butler had brought another dining chair from the nearby room and instructed Lurch to place him upon it and Furtive tied him securely with another length of rope fished from one of his pockets. Taking the opportunity to relax for a few moments, Butler and Furtive sat down with a glass of brandy.

Arthur Milkwood studied the unconscious hunchback. "That's the real Crakett Murdersin, is it?"

"As far as we know," said Butler.

Milkwood looked at Butler hopefully. "Could you do me a favour?"

"If it's to scratch an itch in an embarrassing place, then no, I can't."

Milkwood shook his head. "No, nothing like that. It's just, well, as you mentioned earlier, my performance during this charade has not exactly been of the standing ovation variety, which I once had for my performance of King Leer in Coventry." He paused to glance at Butler and Furtive, but when no form of congratulation was exhibited by either, he continued. "To this end, I believe Crakett's willingness to pay me the fee we agreed on might be a little bit lacking in enthusiasm."

"Quite a bit lacking I should say," said Furtive, puffing on another cigar that had magically appeared.

"I can see how that might be appropriate," agreed Butler.

"I believe this is an ideal opportunity for me to take what is rightly owed, because you see, the fee was not dependent on a successful outcome, but for my services."

"When you say, '*an ideal opportunity,*'" said Butler. "I assume you are alluding to Crakett's unconsciousness and being firmly tied to a chair?"

Milkwood nodded. "I think it is the perfect moment."

"Also, when you said, '*for me to take what is rightly owed*', you actually meant you want me to search through the unconscious hunchback's pockets for any money he may have concealed about his person, and if I find sufficient funds, to take out your fee and stuff it in one of your pockets?"

Again, Milkwood nodded, but added a smile this time. "Plus, any bonus you think I might be entitled to, but I'll leave that to your no doubt kind and generous consideration."

"While you're rummaging through his pockets, Butler, if yer come across his legendary fruit knife, I'll have it," said Furtive. "It'll be a nice little keepsake of this adventure."

"I am not rummaging through anyone's pockets. Your fee, Arthur, is something you'll have to discuss with Crakett later." Butler took a sip of his drink.

"And the fruit knife... is that also off the table?" asked Furtive, hesitantly.

Butler sighed, glanced at the clock and drained his glass. "It's almost midnight. I have to go and fetch Ebenezer." He stood and glanced at the two captives. "Lurch..."

"Oh, it's not more instructions, is it Mr. Butler? It's just I've had so many today my head is spinning."

"I was just going to say what a good job you have done tonight. I am proud of you."

Lurch's smile was so wide it reached behind his ears. "Thank you, Sir. I don't think anyone has ever been proud of me before."

"Well someone is now. I want you to stay in this room and guard the prisoners, can you do that?"

"Of course, Sir, it will be an honour."

Butler turned to Furtive. "You can help Lurch guard our two prisoners and the house while I'm away. Sebastian may yet have another trick or two up his sleeve and there is still Shadow to worry about."

Furtive gave Butler a mock salute. "I'll keep an eye on things, don't yer worry none about that."

Butler plucked the cylinder from the table as he passed. "I don't like leaving both paintings in the same location, so I'll be taking this one with me." He ended the sentence with his eyes resting on Furtive.

Furtive blew out a stream of thick cigar smoke and grinned. "Probably a wise precaution under the circumstances."

"Yes, I thought so." Butler turned and headed toward the door. "I'll be back within the hour."

CHRISTMAS EVE BALL

Earlier, **Ebenezer's first** glimpse of Havasham Hall that night was from the arched glow polluting the night sky. The carriage topped a low hill and there it was in all its glory; in Ebenezer's opinion a slap in the face to decorum. Whereas Ebenezer's house was as brightly lit as a Jewish Christmas tree, Havasham Hall would have made Oxford Street's Christmas lighting displays dim and understated in comparison. One almost needed sunglasses to look in its general direction. So bright was it, the moon sulked.

Butler pulled the carriage to a halt at the end of a line of similar, but in far better condition, conveyances, that stretched out from the building's large columned entrance, emptying their cargo of titled and wealthy passengers. Butler climbed down, opened the carriage door and helped Ebenezer step out.

Ebenezer winced when his feet touched the gravel drive.

"Bunion's playing up, Sir?"

"It's these damn shoes. They are too tight. I should have worn my slippers," he grumbled.

"And how fine they would look with you dressed so smartly in your evening suit. I'm sure all in attendance would have commented on them, Sir."

"Bah! But at least I would have been comfortable."

"Would you like me to escort you inside, Sir?"

"I'm not a child. I can walk to the door unaccompanied."

"As you wish, Sir."

"Anyway, you have much to do tonight. If it all goes to plan, *your plan*, it will be worth all the pain and suffering I will endure this night, and I don't just mean from these damn bunions."

"I'm sure it will, Sir. The only unknown is the full extent of your brother's scheme to acquire your painting."

Ebenezer's stare was both stern and pleading. "He must not get it. I...*we*, will be ruined if he does. You must ensure whatever he has planned fails."

"I will do my best, Sir, of that you can be certain."

"Well, let's hope for both our sakes your best is adequate." Ebenezer turned away and using his cane as support, hobbled as gracefully as he could muster toward the front entrance. "Pick me up at midnight."

Butler watched him go. "Yes, Sir." He climbed onto the carriage, encouraged the two horses to start moving, turned in a wide circle and headed back to Drooge Manor and the forthcoming night's activities.

Ebenezer climbed the marble steps and entered Havasham Hall.

"Oh, look, Ebenezer Drooge has arrived," called out a woman's voice.

Ebenezer handed his hat, coat and gloves to the doorman and turned to see who had mentioned his name. His hosts, Mr. and Mrs. Havasham, walked over with warm smiles on their faces.

Peering over the spectacles balanced on the end of his nose, Mr. Havasham held out a hand. "Ebenezer Drooge, it's wonderful to see you again."

Ebenezer felt obliged to take hold of the offered hand in his bony grasp. "Well, don't think the greeting is mutual. I'm only here because it's a family tradition and not because I find it or the people in attendance particularity pleasurable."

The well-dressed couple laughed.

Mrs. Havasham smiled and grabbed Ebenezer's arm before he could hide it down by his side. "Still the same old grumpy Ebenezer." She led him into the large marbled hallway.

Music and the babble of confused conversation and laughter drifted from the ballroom filled with people drinking, chatting and dancing.

A waiter carrying a tray of drinks balanced on one hand approached. He leaned forward stiffly and proffered the tray at Ebenezer. "Champagne, Sir?"

Ebenezer screwed his nose up at the drink. "I would rather suck the wax from your ears than drink that slop."

"Slop, Sir?" said the waiter in obvious shock. "It's the finest vintage Champagne."

"Vintage slop is what it is. I wouldn't let my toilet drink that muck."

Noticing the waiter's obvious distress, Mrs. Havasham giggled before saving him. "Bring a Brandy for Mr. Drooge, please Jeeves."

"And make sure it's a large one, I think I'll need it."

"Yes, Sir, I will return shortly with your drink." The relieved waiter hurried away.

"I don't think Jeeves has met anyone like you before, Ebenezer. You can be a bit of a shock on a first encounter."

"Not just the first," added Mr. Havasham with a smile.

"What do you think of the house this year, Ebenezer?" asked Mrs. Havasham.

"Even more gaudy and eye offensive as last year's, something I thought impossible until seeing it."

She giggled.

"I tell you, if a man was on the moon and looked back toward earth, he would notice two things: this carbuncle of a house standing out like a blemish of good taste, and that huge offensive excuse for a nose in the centre of your otherwise pretty face."

The couple laughed.

"Come on, Sebastian, my wife's nose isn't that big. I find it rather cute."

"Then, Havasham, I suggest you get some stronger lenses for your rose-tinted spectacles."

Mrs. Havasham grabbed both his hands. "I simply love your humour. I'll share something with you, Ebenezer..."

"If it's the name of the bloke who did your garish party lights, don't bother. He should by hung by a string of his own lights for his profanity against nature and good taste."

Mrs. Havasham laughed again. "What I was going to say before I was so jovially interrupted, was meeting you at this annual gathering is the highlight of my year."

Ebenezer snorted. "If your life truly is that depressing, I'd think about making a few drastic changes."

She laughed and grabbed one of his cheeks between delicate fingers and gave it a wobble. "I could hug you for making me laugh so much."

"Please don't. You'd likely take out an eye with that dagger-like appendage."

She laughed again and linked her arm back in his.

Jeeves intercepted them. "Your brandy, Sir."

Ebenezer turned to the waiter, took the glass and stared suspiciously at the drink. "Is that a double?"

"It is in polite society, Sir," answered the waiter with forced civility.

"In that case, bring me two more in the same glass."

"Of course, Sir. Two double brandy's in a glass not fashioned to hold them."

"You can pour them in a bucket for all I care," said Ebenezer.

The waiter glared as civilly as he was able as he backed away a few steps before spinning away and disappeared into the crowd.

"So, Ebenezer, not with your brother tonight?" enquired Mr. Havasham.

"I haven't associated with my brother for nigh on thirty years, why would you possibly think our estrangement would suddenly change?"

"Exactly!" stated Mr. Havasham. "Thirty years is a long time for this rift between you to continue."

"Bah! If I live for another thirty, which I very much doubt, the rift will remain for what he has done."

"But..."

His wife placed a hand on her husband's arm to silence him. "Let us not talk of such things at such a joyous time of year. Ebenezer, will you honour me with a dance later?"

He shrugged. "If my bunions are behaving themselves, I suppose we can stumble around the dance floor."

She smiled and laid a hand on his arm. "It's a date then?"

"I said so, didn't I?"

She laughed, grabbed her husband's arm and led him away. "I simply love that man."

"Ebenezer," called out a voice he recognized and despised.

Ignoring the voice, Ebenezer drained his glass and hoping to spy the waiter returning with his fresh drink, glanced around at the crowd; there was no sign of him. He reluctantly focused on his approaching nemesis who was accompanied by two ladies, one on each arm.

Sebastian grinned. "You made it then, brother?"

"Obviously." Ebenezer turned his attention to the two identical twins. They were pretty and a lot younger than Sebastian. "I didn't realize you had started a babysitting service, or are they your daughters I never knew you had?"

The girls giggled.

"See, ladies, I told you my brother was funny. Ebenezer let me introduce you to my beautiful companions."

Ebenezer sighed in a bored fashion. "If you must."

"On my left arm is Miss Abigail Fortune and on my right, her sister, Miss Wendy Fortune, daughters of Sir Jerrymire Fortune, the well-known wealthy industrialist and banker."

"Never heard of him," said Ebenezer, curtly.

"Well known that is, in the top end of society, which I am afraid, my brother, is a height you could never hope to climb to."

"If you are part of it I'd rather not make the effort."

Sebastian glanced around and then back at his brother. "On your own again, I see."

"I am quite content with my own company and, unlike most people, have no desire to fill it with trinkets of companionship." His eyes glanced at the two Fortune sisters. "You two shouldn't be hanging around with this old relic, but with someone nearer your own age."

"Sebastian was kind enough to give us a lift," explained Abigail.

Sebastian merely smiled. "Okay, girls, why don't you go show yourselves off. I am sure there are many young suitable men here who would welcome the chance of sharing a dance with two stunning beauties like you two."

The girls giggled, detached themselves from Sebastian's arms and, hand in innocent hand, entered the ballroom where they were greeted by many pairs of appreciative eyes.

"So, Ebenezer, how are things at dreary Drooge Manor?"

"Everything is shipshape and secure as my crumbling mansion can be. And what about Castle Gloom?"

"Likewise, but even more secure than you or that manservant of yours could ever imagine. A mouse, however *furtive*, would not be able to gain entry."

Ebenezer smiled. *His brother thought his knowledge of the burglar was a surprise.* "Furtive is as furtive does," he replied confidently.

Puzzled by the comment. Sebastian stared at his brother suspiciously. "I have no idea what that means."

Ebenezer pondered his recent remark. He had no idea either, but he wasn't about to admit it. Trusting a confident smile would get him out of trouble, he brought one to his lips.

"I think old age and that damp hovel you live in has taken its toll on your faculties, brother."

Seizing upon the chance to parry a retort in their game of words, Ebenezer put a hand to his back. "I think you are right brother, my back is steadily become more *hunched*, I fear soon I will resemble *Quasimodo*." Ebenezer enjoyed the brief flash of surprise upon his brother' face.

Recovering quickly from his brother's unexpected revelation, Sebastian's confident expression reformed. *Ebenezer knew about the Crakett Murdersin, not that it would do him any good. My precautions are too protective and encompassing for even the remotest chance of any scheme devised by my brother and that butler of his to succeed. But did he know about my plan of attack? I have to find out.* "It is true; you are becoming a *shadow* of your former self." The lack of any recognition shown by his brother at the mention of Shadow inspired confidence Ebenezer was ignorant of the thief-assassin in his employ. The painting was as good as his, and with it his grandfather's inheritance.

Though the confident smile remained on Ebenezer's lips, his thoughts were confused and worried. Why did my brother emphasize the word, shadow? What possible repercussions could it have for a successful outcome of my venture already set into motion? Whatever it is, I'm powerless to do anything about it other than pray Butler handles whatever surprise s thrown in his path.

"Your brandy, Sir."

Grateful for the distraction, Ebenezer took the offered brandy and placed the empty glass on the tray.

"Is your drink in order this time, Sir?" enquired Jeeves with a barely disguised sarcastic overtone.

Ebenezer studied the large glass filled to the brim with the delicious brown liquid. He smiled at the waiter. "Excellent, Jeeves, well done."

Taken aback by the unexpected compliment, Jeeves turned to Sabastian. "Champagne, Sir?"

Sebastian took a glass. "Vintage, Jeeves?"

"Extremely, Sir." The waiter shot a glance at Ebenezer before disappearing into the crowd.

Ebenezer stared confidently into his brother's eyes and just as confidently his brother's eyes stared back. He held up his glass. "The games have begun, brother."

Sebastian smiled. "They certainly have."

"To the winner," toasted Ebenezer.

"To the winner," Sebastian repeated, having no doubts it would be him.

The two men brought their glasses together briefly, took a sip, turned and walked away from each other as if they were fighting a duel. Though they shared glances across the room, no more words passed between them for the rest of the night.

Butler drove the carriage past those lined up in front of the mansion and reined the horses to a halt in front of the entrance. Ebenezer and Mrs. Havasham waited at the top of the steps. He also noticed the relief on his master's face on seeing him arrive.

Relieved he could leave and find out how things went tonight, Ebenezer turned to his host. "As usual, Agnus, it's been a thoroughly unpleasant experience and now, thankfully, it is time for me to leave."

Mrs. Havasham, much to Ebenezer's annoyance, linked her arm through his and accompanied down the steps.

She smiled fondly at Ebenezer. "Will you be back next year?"

"If I'm not a corpse by then, I might."

She laughed. "The way you whisked me around that dance floor for most of the night, I'm sure you will outlive us all, Ebenezer."

"It's not something I'd admit in public, but you are an excellent dancer and the time we spent together wasn't totally abhorrent, almost enjoyable."

Mrs. Havasham laughed. "Then I'm glad the evening has not been completely unpleasant for you. And don't forget what I said, Ebenezer, you know where I live, you can come and visit at any time."

"I wouldn't hold your breath on that score, and don't forget what I said, you come calling on me and I'll set the dogs on you."

"You don't have any dogs." Again, she laughed." I'll miss your wit and the man that is you, Ebenezer." She stroked a hand gently on his cheek. "You need to find yourself a wife to care for you."

"Bah! What do I want one of those for? I have Butler to look after me."

Butler opened the door of the carriage. "It is my life's burden, Sir."

"No, not inside, Butler, we need to talk. I'll sit up beside you."

Butler helped Ebenezer up into the driver's seat and fetched the blanket from inside to wrap around him.

"Make sure you take good care of him, Butler," said Mrs. Havasham.

Butler nodded. "I do try, Mrs. Havasham, but it's not always easy." He climbed onto the seat next to Ebenezer and clucked the horses into motion.

"Good bye, Ebenezer, don't be a stranger," called out Mrs. Havasham.

He flashed a weak but warm smile. "Thanks for the evening, Agnes, it was okay, really."

She smiled warmly and waited until the carriage had turned and headed up the long driveway before returning, a little hesitantly it seemed, inside.

Butler glanced at the house as they drove by and noticed Sebastian watching them from one of the windows.

"Now Butler, tell me how your evening went."

"Well, Sir, it wasn't without its problems, but I am happy to report, so far it has been successful."

"We have Sebastian's painting?" Ebenezer asked excitedly.

"Yes, Sir, we most definitely do."

"Well done, Butler. This is wonderful news."

"We couldn't have done it without Furtive, Sir. I think you should give him the original ten thousand as planned."

"Yes, okay, I suppose he earned it."

"He undoubtedly did, Sir."

Ebenezer rubbed his hands together gleefully. "Sebastian is going to be livid when he finds out."

"That's not going to be a problem, is it, Sir? He doesn't seem the type to forgive and forget, especially with what's at stake."

Ebenezer shrugged. "It's difficult to know for certain, but there are unwritten rules to the game we play, and he must accept that I have won, and he has lost."

"Hmmm," mumbled Butler. "Might I inquire who wrote these unwritten rules, Sir?"

"Well, no one really, we both sort of assumed they were part of our game."

"Was it both or just *you*, Sir, who assumed this?"

"I assumed he had also assumed there were certain rules."

"Ah, forgive my lack of confidence in your brother's gamesmanship, but I believe when he discovers we have stolen his painting, the only rules he will be playing by will be his own."

As Butler steered the horses through the wide gateway of Havasham Hall and onto the track leading to the Drooge estate, snow began to fall. He looked to the east at the brooding dark clouds creeping past a sulky moon. "A storm is coming, Sir."

Ebenezer continued to stare straight ahead and pulled the blanket tighter around him. "Yes, I know."

After a while of brooding silence, Ebenezer spoke. "Will we be okay, Butler?"

Butler looked at his frail master. "Yes, I am sure we will, Sir."

"Good... I want you to know that even if it doesn't seem so at times, I do look upon you as a friend."

"Thank you, Sir, and at times, like right now for example, the feeling is mutual."

After a few moments silence, Butler spoke. "Sir, can I ask you a question? It's a bit personal and I would like to know, but if you don't want to answer I'll understand."

Ebenezer turned his head to look at Butler, but said nothing for a few moments. "Alright, but if I answer your question you must answer mine."

"Agreed, Sir. This rift with your brother, how did it start?"

Ebenezer sighed, as if hesitant to answer. "As you are aware, Butler, I am not one to open up to my feelings easily, but we have known each other for a long time now, almost twenty years, so I will give you your answer. It started with a young lady called Nancy. In the scheme of things, she was no one special, she worked in the tavern her parents owned in a town not far from here, but she was very special to me. I loved her. I know you probably think a man like me is incapable of such an emotion, but I wasn't always the bitter miser you have known me to be. Nancy and I had been on a few dates and we had kissed, but I wanted more. I wanted to spend the rest of my life with her. I wanted her to be my wife. I bought a ring, nothing fancy, but as much as I could afford at the time. Sebastian noticed me looking at it one day and I foolishly told him my plans. In two days' time I had arranged to meet Nancy and was going to ask her to marry me. It was a mistake I regret to this day.

"Sebastian, a year younger and the better-looking brother, always desired what I had, even if he didn't want it; toys, school friends and the like. I should have realized the thing I most desired in the world he would also want to take from me. The day arrived when I was to meet with Nancy and propose, but when I arrived at the inn she wasn't there. I waited for hours, but she didn't return. The following day I saw her walking through town hand in hand with my brother, talking and laughing. When my brother noticed me across the street, he took her in his arms and kissed her. I couldn't bear it. I ran with tears streaming from my eyes and my heart in pieces.

"A few weeks later I discovered she was pregnant and, of course, Sebastian wanted nothing to do with her after that. He told me he was bored with her and I could have her back if I wanted. Nancy came to see me. She cried and said she was sorry and told me when she had told Sebastian she was having his baby and that he had to marry her, he told her he wanted nothing to do with her and she should ask me because I had planned to ask her to marry me a few weeks before. The courage of the girl to come and ask that very thing of me after she had broken my heart was remarkable. It showed how desperate she was. The shame of having a baby out of wedlock was more than she could bear. I was angry and slammed the door in her face. Two days later she took her own life. I have never forgiven myself for turning her away and I will never, as long as I draw breath, forgive my brother. It was this that changed me and started the rift between us." He looked at the man sitting next to him. "Does that answer your question?"

Butler nodded sadly. "I'm sorry, Sir. I didn't realize."

"No one does."

After a few moments, Ebenezer spoke again. "My question for you, Butler, is why are you here? Why have you stayed with me for so long? I have known a few butlers in my time and none were like you. You could easily find a comfortable position somewhere a lot plusher than Drooge Manor, with a far less demanding master and be paid a lot more, so why do you stay with me? I know you don't like talking about yourself, which is why I know as much about you now as I did when you first arrived, and I respect that, but I would like to know."

"It's true, Sir, when I advertised in the newspapers for a position, you were not the only reply I had, and yes, I could have chosen a position in a grand house full of servants, the offers were there, but you were different. They only wanted me, but you *needed* me, and I wasn't sure you would survive if I didn't accept your offer of employment. That is why I came and why I remain with you." He looked at Ebenezer. "Now you know, Sir?"

Ebenezer nodded and used the blanket to wipe his eyes. "Damn that cold wind. It's causing my eyes water."

"I know, Sir. I have mentioned this before, but you do realize I can't stay forever. I have lived your life for almost twenty years and though I don't regret a day of it, well perhaps a few, I need to start living one of my own."

Ebenezer remained silent, glanced into the sky and watched the snowflakes drift from the heavens. A few moments later he sat up straighter. "That's enough of all this maudlin talk. Tell me exactly what happened while I was at that ghastly ball."

"I'm sure it wasn't all ghastly, Sir. Mrs. Havasham obviously likes you, though God knows why the way you speak to her."

"I make her laugh. I'm not sure she gets much chance to laugh with all those high and mighty posh friends of hers; some of them are so stuck up they'd drown in a rainstorm without an umbrella, so when I meet her each year I make an extra effort to give her a good time. It's the only reason I go."

"Sir, I think you just brought a tear to my eye."

"Probably that cold wind or a flake of snow."

"If you say so, Sir."

"Okay, tell me what happened, every detail mind."

"When I returned to the manor after dropping you at Havasham Hall, I took the horses and carriage to the stable and..."

"...Not every damn detail, blast you man, just the good bits relevant to the crime."

Butler grinned. "Yes, Sir. I returned to the Manor and..."

By the time Ebenezer and Butler arrived home, Ebenezer had heard the full story. He was astonished on hearing there was a third Hunchback and that the real one and Arthur were tied up in his manor. He was also impressed with everyone's role in the successful outcome.

Lurch and Furtive greeted Ebenezer when he entered his study. After a glance at the unconscious Crakett and Arthur Milkwood, he headed for the sofa to rest his tired feet. Before he had finished making himself comfortable, Furtive was handing him a glass of brandy at arm's length with his head turned away. Ebenezer took a sip and looked at Furtive. "Butler said you are to be congratulated on your performance tonight, well done and be assured there will be a considerable bonus coming your way."

Furtive smiled and nodded appreciatively. "Thanks Ebenezer."

"Um, did Butler happen to mention my performance?" asked Milkwood hopefully.

"Not in any words that could be confused to be those of praise or inspire me or your employer, I should think, to be issuing any bonuses in your direction."

"Oh."

Butler entered with a steaming bowl of hot water emitting the scent of mustard. He placed it on the floor beside Ebenezer, pulled the man's shoes and socks off, rolled up his trouser legs and pulled the bowl nearer. "Careful, Sir, it's a tad hot."

Ebenezer let out a satisfied sigh as he slowly lowered his feet into the hot mustard water. "Ahhhhhh! Just what the doctor ordered."

"Um, not really, Sir. If I recall, he said, 'plunging your bunions into hot water could cause them to swell and explode like a puss-filled hand grenade.'"

"Bah! Doctors, what do they know? All they want to do is charge exorbitant fees for a poke and a prod and a taking of temperature and then they have the gall to demand a king's ransom for a tiny bottle of potion, poultice or sachet of powder. They are all thieves and charlatans, every damn one."

"If you say so, Sir."

"By the way, Butler, thank you for the foot bath," he mumbled.

Butler's eyebrows rose without any encouragement. "My, you are in a good mood, Sir."

Ebenezer shrugged. "I don't suppose it will last."

"No, Sir, that's as certain as the sun rising in the morning."

Ebenezer glanced over at the prisoners. "What's your plan for them two?"

Butler joined his gaze. "I was thinking we leave them tied up until we have found, you know what, and then when it's safe to do so, we set them free."

"That seems best and I can't see an alternative."

"Well I certainly can," argued Milkwood. "I understand why you wouldn't want to let Crakett go just yet, but me, I'm no threat to you, so why not let me go now?"

"And what's to stop you from returning to untie Crakett? He was the one that hired you and you have shown an eagerness to be paid, deserved or not."

"After my dismal performance tonight, do you really think I'd set him free when I'm close by? I might as well cut my own throat. But, I will admit, if you did let me go I was going to return when you had gone, but not to set him free..."

"...you want to go through his pockets to get your money," stated Furtive.

Milkwood nodded. "But if you are not happy with that, you could always pay me what I'm owed and then I'd have no reason to return. I'd go to the nearest town and wait for the morning train and then I'd be gone."

"No, you are staying put until we have completed our mission," Butler told him. "We still don't know if you are who you say you are?"

In an exaggerated frustrated manner, Milkwood sagged his shoulders as much as the ropes would allow, and huffed.

"Lurch, I want you to go upstairs..." Ebenezer sighed. "Not yet."

Lurch re-entered the room. "Sorry, Sir."

"Wait until I finish speaking before you leave."

"Yes, Sir. Sorry, Sir. Have you finished now?"

"No! I want you to go upstairs and keep an eye on the castle through the telescope and let me know when Sebastian's carriage returns, or anything unusual happens. Do you understand?"

Lurch nodded doubtfully.

"Good, now you can leave."

Lurch left the room. Every one of his footsteps across the hall, up the stairs, along the landing and into the telescope room could be heard.

Crakett Murdersin drowsily opened his eyes and scanned everyone in the room. His gaze ended on Butler. "You haven't killed me, I see."

"Oh, they wouldn't do something like that, Mr. Murdersin," said Milkwood. "They are quite nice actually. Butler and Ebenezer are like an old married couple and Lurch is a bit dim, but kind hearted, I think. The only one to watch out for is the foul one over there smoking the cigar, his breath smells like..."

Crakett glared at Furtive. "...Yes, we've met, and I have, to my detriment, experienced the foulness of its potent stench. It's not something I, my lungs, or my nose will forget in a hurry."

Furtive smiled. "As you see, Crakett, the advantage is no longer yours."

"Looks can sometimes be deceiving," replied Crakett.

Furtive plucked the pistol from his lap and aimed it at Crakett. "But not in this particular case."

"Well, no, maybe not in this particular case, but sometimes they can be. When I am free, be assured I will kill you very slowly and in a manner excruciatingly unpleasant."

Furtive smiled. "Not a very sensible thing to say to someone who has low morals and a loaded weapon trained on your heart while you are bound to a chair."

"Not really, but it felt good."

Butler entered, picked up the pistol from the table and approached Crakett. "Goodnight Mr. Murdersin." He swiped him around the head with the pistol butt. Crakett's head sagged to his chest.

Butler turned to Milkwood.

Milkwood cowered. "Please don't hit me. My face is my profession."

"Remain quiet and behave yourself and I'll have no reason to." Butler glanced at Ebenezer and smiled. He had fallen asleep. *The dancing must have tired him out.*

Furtive stared at the red welt on Crakett's temple starting to swell. "Why'd yer knock him out?"

"We are relocating to the dining room to examine the paintings and thought it unwise to leave Crakett alone in here lest he escaped."

"Fair point," Furtive agreed.

Though a little upset no one thought him capable of escaping or a threat that needed a hard, sharp blow to the head, Milkwood thought it wise he sulked in silence.

Butler gently lifted Ebenezer.

Furtive reached for the brandy decanter on the coffee table.

"Leave it," ordered Butler. You'll need a clear head for what I believe is coming our way." With Ebenezer cradled in his arms, Butler left the room.

Furtive drained his glass, placed it beside the decanter and followed Butler.

Shadow, who had been in the room observing the goings on of the eccentric group and had heard and seen all, contemplated what to do next. Shadow's gaze focused on Butler as he crossed the room with the old man in his arms. *They were a strange partnership, Butler and Ebenezer. Arthur was correct when he said they were like an old married couple. Both had a fondness for each other, but both were too embarrassed to show it to any great extent.* After a glance at the bound prisoners, Shadow slipped silently from the room.

Butler crossed to the dining room but paused when Lurch came down the stairs and halted on the half landing with a worried frown at seeing his master in Butler arms.

"Has he gone, Sir?" he asked, sadly.

Butler shook his head. "Just asleep." Sensing Lurch had more to say, he said, "What is it Lurch?"

"Sebastian's carriage has just turned toward the castle."

"Thank you. Return to your lookout and let me know if you notice any other activity around the castle. If you do, let me know immediately."

"I will do, Sir." To avoid disturbing his master, Lurch crept up the stairs as quietly as his large bulk and feet would allow.

Butler carried Ebenezer into the dining room.

14th
CHAPTER

TWO BECOME
ONE

Now **wide awake**, slippers on his feet and sitting in his rickety wheelchair, Ebenezer's excited eyes observed Butler and Furtive spreading out the two paintings on the dining table. "I have waited so long for this moment I can hardly believe happening."

"We still have to solve your grandfather's clues, Sir. Your father spent his whole life trying without success."

"Yes, but he didn't have you, Butler. I am confident you will solve them."

The three men studied the paintings, glancing from one to the other. Though similar, both had their differences. Both were views of the desolate moor and both featured Drooge Manor and Castle Drooge in the background. In Ebenezer's painting the Manor was on the left and the Castle on the right, in Sebastian's they were reversed. In the foreground of both paintings there was a pile of square-edged moss-covered rocks, partially overgrown with grass, and weeds with unusual white flowers, behind them was a large bush. Though a piece of jewellery, a strange ring set with a single ruby, appeared in both paintings, their positions were also reversed.

Ebenezer pointed at the ring in one of the paintings. "I think the ring has to indicate the treasure."

"It's possible," commented Butler, deep in thought. "But what puzzles me is why some of the details in each picture are reversed; they have to be clues as they are the only differences between them."

"Maybe it's a view of the same thing but from a different angle?" suggested Furtive. "Like a front and back view."

"We have checked," said Butler. "There is no location you can stand around here to get this view of both the Manor and the Castle, whichever way around they are positioned."

Butler tried arranging the paintings end to end, side to side and upside down to each other, but still nothing made sense. "It's as I thought, the clues are not going to be easy to solve."

"I know we've checked the back of my painting, but is there anything that may help us on the back of Sebastian's," asked Ebenezer.

Butler flipped the painting over, laying it on top of the other so Ebenezer could get a good look.

Ebenezer scrutinized the aged canvas. "Nothing! It's as bare as my bank balance. Flip it back over."

Butler gripped one end and pulled it back.

"Stop!" shouted Furtive.

Butler and Ebenezer stared at the man standing a short distance from the table.

Furtive pointed at the raised painting edge Butler held. "Lower it down slowly, I thought I saw something." He guided Butler with slow movements of his hand until half of Ebenezer's painting was covered by Sebastian's. "That's it, hold it there."

Butler held the painting steady and tried to look at what Furtive gazed at so intensely, but from his position he couldn't see what it was.

Furtive pointed out something. "Do yer see that, Ebenezer?"

Ebenezer clamped a hand firmly over his nose and leaned forward for a better view. "I see nothing I've not seen before."

"You have ter look at the two halves of the paintings as one. Concentrate on the two rubies and tell me what they look like?"

Ebenezer looked at both precious stones. "They look a bit like eyes, I suppose."

"Exactly! Now look at the outer edges of the bushes in each painting and tell us what yer see?"

Ebenezer cocked his head from side to side. "Ears, perhaps?"

"Good. If the rubies are eyes and the edge of the bushes the ears..." Furtive pointed a grubby finger at the bottom section of the painting,

"...what are these strange flowering weeds down here?"

Ebenezer peered at the shrubbery and suddenly saw the whole picture. He turned to Furtive. "Oh my god, Furtive, you've cracked it. I know where the treasure is. If your breath didn't smell fouler than a potato so rotten it's turned to liquid, I'd hug you."

"Thank you, Mr. Ebenezer, but I'd rather yer show yer appreciation with an increase in that bonus yer mentioned earlier," said Furtive hopefully.

The smile dropped from Ebenezer's lips. "Let's not be too hasty with the dishing out of bonuses just yet. That time might come when I have the treasure in my hands."

"Then I will be sure to ask again when yer 'ave."

"Excuse me for interrupting your celebrations, Sir, but what exactly has Furtive found to make you think you know where your grandfather's inheritance is hidden?"

Furtive took the painting from Butler and folded the top painting over on itself. After he had made a few adjustments, he stood back. "Now, Butler, what do yer see?"

At first Butler saw nothing, but when he studied what Furtive had said about the eyes and ears, an image formed. "Could it be so simple?" he questioned.

"It would explain that strange clause in Jacobus's will," said Ebenezer.

"What clause would that be, Sir?"

Ebenezer explained. "The clause states the castle could only be owned by a Drooge, that the owner must feed Diablo every day and if the food remained un-eaten for longer than two weeks, an indication it was probably dead, a message must be sent to the address included in the clause and a replacement would be brought. Failure to adhere to any stipulations in this clause would result in the family member responsible being turned out of the castle without a penny and with only the clothes on their back. It even includes a failsafe if the Drooge family line died out."

"Jacobus hid his wealth in the quarry knowing no one would dare enter because of Diablo."

"Exactly!" said Ebenezer. "It's the perfect hiding place and Diablo is the perfect guardian."

"I've been in the quarry," said Furtive. "I didn't see much of it, but it seemed a big area, it won't be easy ter find."

"That's where you are wrong, Furtive. I know exactly where it is." Ebenezer tapped the image of the red eyed wolf baring its fangs. "Diablo's lair!"

Butler stared at the scary image. "I suppose the reversed manor and castle was the clue to match them together. Here like this," he pointed to the painting, "the two castles are on top of each other and folded back it reveals the wolf image.

It's so vague if Furtive hadn't glimpsed something we may never have worked it out."

Ebenezer smiled at the burglar. "Well done Furtive."

"I wonder what we'll see if we put the two Drooge Manors together and fold the other half of the painting back?"

"Good point, Butler," said Ebenezer. "Do it."

Butler flipped the folded painting over, repositioned it on the other half of the painting and matched up the two manors.

All three stared at the image and though there seemed to be something there, none of them could work out what it was.

Butler tilted his head to the side and thought he saw something. He grabbed the paintings and turned them upside down and slowly the details faded together.

Two dark patches in the rocks became eye sockets with a single white bloom in their centres; an outcrop of rock became a nose and a fissure was now lips. Clumps of bushes become ears and moss became a beard.

Ebenezer and Butler glanced at the portrait on the wall.

"It's Jacobus!" stated Ebenezer.

Unlike the stern features of the man's likeness in the portrait, his image in the painting smirked at them.

Lurch shouted down the staircase. "Sir, I think we might have a problem."

Butler rushed to the window. In the distance a group of men stampeded along the road toward the Manor. At a less-hurried gait followed a lone man; Sebastian. "Furtive, do you have a pair of binoculars?"

"I'm a thief, ain't I? Course I have binoculars." He thrust a hand into a pocket and rummaged around. "Any particular make or magnification?"

Butler looked at the thief. "The strongest you have."

Furtive pulled out a small red pair. "Oops, they are me opera glasses." His hand returned to his pocket.

"You go to the opera?" asked Butler, in surprise.

"Only to find out what toffs aren't home, so I can break into their house and rob 'em."

"I suppose that makes sense and rather clever. I'm surprised you aren't a rich thief by now." Butler took the next pair of binoculars to appear in Furtive's hand, turned to the window and put them to his eyes.

"It's me own fault I'm not. Drink and gambling is my curse. I spend quicker than I can steal."

Butler focused in on the men; all were heavily armed. He repositioned his view upon Sebastian. His face, a mask of angry determination, informed Butler if Sebastian had previously worn gloves, they were now definitely off.

Ebenezer rolled his wheelchair to the window. "What do you see, Butler?"

"Nothing good, Sir. Your brother and his men are coming, and I fear this time they won't stop until they have the paintings."

Ebenezer decisively grabbed his painting from the table and threw it into the fireplace. The oil paint blistered and burst into flame as the fire hungrily began to devour it.

Butler's brow creased in a frown. "Perhaps not the wisest move, Sir. If your grandfather's inheritance is not where you think it is there will be no second chance to find it."

"It's there, Butler. I've never been more certain of anything in my life. I can't believe I didn't think of it before. " Ebenezer grabbed Sebastian's painting and gave it to Butler. "Return this to my brother; it may quell his thirst for revenge."

"Without yours to accompany it, I find that very doubtful, Sir." Butler opened the window, threw the painting out and closed it. "I suggest we make sure the prisoners are secure and let Sebastian deal with them, and move ourselves out of harm's way through the secret tunnel."

"And then we go and find Jacobus's long-lost inheritance," added Ebenezer.

"Lurch, we won't be able to take the wheelchair."

"No problem, Sir, he's not heavy. I'll carry him." He lifted his master from the chair and put him on his back.

"I'm not a sack of coal, be a bit gentler with my old body."

"Sorry, Sir."

"Okay, let's get going before our uninvited guests arrive." Butler led them from the room.

Ben Hammott

15th
CHAPTER

ESCAPE AND
RESCUE

Butler, with lantern in hand and a fast pace to his feet, led the oddball group down the steps and across the rickety bridge.

Shadow, who was only a few steps behind them, had decided to follow and take charge of as large a portion of the treasure as it was possible for one person to carry when it was found.

Their dash through the underground realm was a wise move.

Though not totally unexpected, when Sebastian had gone to his hidden museum to check all was in order and discovered the room absent its hunchback guardian and his painting stolen, the man was outraged. When he set his art-appreciative eyes upon the painting that had replaced his, the amateurish grotesque rendering of his brother's naked butt violated his mind, body and soul. Any unwritten rules that may have existed were torn to shreds and promptly burnt. With a face as red and angry as the boil festering on his brother's butt cheek that recently stared out at him from the picture a moment ago, Sebastian had stormed from the room.

Though Flint Stone and his men had expected their employer to return in a good mood, a smile on his lips and generous thoughts of handing out Christmas bonuses for a job well executed, as soon as they saw the manic look upon his face all thoughts of praise and bonuses of any description quickly evaporated.

Fuming, Sebastian paused in the doorway and glared fiercely at the anxious expressions of his employees.

When after a few moments he had still not said anything, Flint asked the worst question he possibly could in the current situation. "Is everything alright, Sebastian?"

Slowly Sebastian turned his head to stare at Flint. "IS EVERYTHING ALRIGHT! Hold on, let me see. I return home from a not too entertaining party to discover the one thing I had spared no expense to protect, including the hiring of the eight men in this room I spent money on training, a hunchback who came highly recommended, arranged security a flea would have trouble passing through, and yet, despite all these precautions the impossible has happened; my painting has been stolen."

Flint glanced at the rolled canvass held in his employer's hand. "Stolen, Sir, are you sure?"

As you can tell by his latest inquiry, Flint is at the top of his class when it comes to choosing questions that should not be asked.

"AM I SURE!"

Though Flint tried to ignore the smoke whooshing out of his employer's ears, it was so fascinating he couldn't help but stare.

"OF COURSE I'M DAMN SURE!"

He unrolled the painting and held it up for all in the corridor to see.

The effect of the shocked gasp travelling the length of the room was spoilt by the man at the back, yes, Figgins again, who screwed up his eyes to get a better look at the painting.

"Is that an elephant?" He used his recently cleaned pistol to point at certain details, which caused all those directly in its path to duck. "I can make out the long trunk and its large left eye, but the right pink one seems too small and too centralized." His gun waved to the right. "It should be over a bit."

The man directly in front, leaned forward and whispered in the art critic's ear the exact nature of the painted image.

The man was so shocked his finger tensed on the trigger. A gunshot echoed through the corridor. A bullet sped down its length, went through the painting and whizzed past Sebastian's ear.

Sebastian put his eye to the hole and peered through at the man who had fired the shot.

Figgins quickly hid the smoking weapon behind his back and stared at the eye peering through the hole his bullet had made through the detail he had believed to be a small pink eye.

"Erh! That's very disturbing. Does anyone else find that rather creepy?"

The others stared at the eye the far side of the hole that blinked, and though all thought it was the creepiest thing they had ever seen, they kept their opinions to themselves.

In an attempt to restore some sort of order to the proceedings, Flint took it upon himself to ask another of his questions that should never be asked. "So, Mr. Sebastian, this painting is definitely not your missing artwork?"

The eye looked at Flint. Slowly the offensive image was lowered. "Is the repulsive subject portrayed so amateurishly here look like something I would own?"

Flint, forever one to push his luck, shrugged. "Not knowing you very well, Mr. Sabastian, or indeed any peculiar tastes you may have, I find your question impossible to answer. But be assured, none of us here are passing judgment. We all have different tastes in art. Now me, I like a nice landscape, but I know people who..."

"SHUT UP!"

"Of course, Sir. Shutting up immediately."

Sebastian threw the painting to the ground. "If I don't get my painting back, deaths will occur. Do I make myself perfectly clear?" His gaze looked at each man in turn until it fell upon the man at the back who had raised a hand. Sebastian sighed. "It was a rhetorical question, Figgins."

"Oh, yes, Sir, I understand that alright. It was about the painting why I raised my weaponless arm. I was wondering like, that if you don't want it, could I have it?" He looked at his angry employer hopefully.

"Ignore him, Sir, he's an idiot." Flint stepped in front of Sebastian to block his view of the man. "We understand your orders completely, Sir, and they will be obeyed," he stated confidently.

With a puzzled expression professionally painted upon his face, Sebastian tilted his head to the side so he could peer around Flint and see the idiot at the end of the room again. "You really like the painting?"

Figgins nodded enthusiastically. "Oh, yes, Sir, I really do. It's got a certain appeal I can't quite work out and I am certain the wife will love it. It'll look great in a nice frame. We always wanted a nice bit of art to hang on the wall, a sort of talking piece for when we have guests, like."

Sebastian shook his head in amazement. "There is no accounting for some people's taste. Flint, pick it up and give it to the art blind idiot, the farther it is away from my sight the better."

"Yes, Sir." Flint picked up the painting and passed it to the man behind him. "Pass it along lads."

Held between two fingers and with eyes averted from the unholy image, the painting was passed back to the man with extremely bad taste in art.

Figgins proudly took charge of the canvas and rolled it up. "Thank you, Sir."

Sebastian dismissed the thanks with a casual wave of the hand and turned to his second in command. "Maybe I was hearing things, Flint, but I am certain a moment ago you informed me, quite confidently as I recall, that you all understood my orders and would obey them."

"One hundred percent correct, Sir. We are to find and return to you your painting that in no way resembles a degusting, deformed queer eyed elephant."

Sebastian placed his hands behind his back, grasped them together and leaned forward. "And yet, here you all stand. Is your plan to wait here for the thief to bring back my painting and hand it to you?"

Flint smirked. "No, Sir, I think that's highly unlikely."

Sebastian shook his head. "Now I am seeing things, because if that is a real smile on your lips, I will cut them off and make you eat them."

Flint's smile disappeared. "Not a smile, Sir. Definitely not a smile." He spun to face the others in the room. "Okay, men, on the double now, let's go and get Mr. Sebastian's painting back for him."

Keen to be away from Sebastian's wrath, the men poured through the far exit.

"I'll be having a drinks party next week if anyone wants to come," said Figgins.

No one accepted the invitation.

"I don't care how you do it or who gets harmed in the process, I want my painting, as well as Ebenezer's, in my hands before the sun rises!"

"Yes, Sir, we'll do our best," called out Flint, a moment before he rushed through the far door.

Sebastian followed at a slower pace and attempted to piece together what had taken place that night. It was obvious now that Crakett worked for my brother. But what about Shadow? Where did the assassin thief's loyalties lie? I must assume the worst; Shadow cannot be relied upon. They would all die for their deceit, but how can this and the retrieval of the paintings be achieved? My incompetent men were no match for the skills of Crakett and Shadow and perhaps even the Furtive thief, Ebenezer had hired. Or was that just a ploy to distract me. And how did the hunchback manage to climb up the narrow chimney? Even more of a mystery is how could the person who painted that evil picture stare at his brother's disgusting rear end long enough to record its details onto canvas? Nothing made sense anymore. There was only one thing I can do. I'll have to take control.

With vengeance guiding his thoughts, Sebastian strode along the corridor and up the stairs.

Butler entered the secret rooms below the manor and led the group across the wooden path and into the old underground study. He kicked the mildewed armchair aside, tore back the rotten rug and knelt to raise the trapdoor hidden beneath. He held up the lamp and told Furtive to enter. "It only leads in one direction, so you can't get lost."

Furtive lit and slipped on his head lantern before clambering down the steep stone steps.

"Butler gently lifted Ebenezer off Lurch's back and waited while Lurch squeezed his large bulk through the small opening."

"Isn't this exciting, Butler. Just what the doctor ordered."

"Um, no, not really, Sir. If I recall, what the doctor actually said when he took your pulse, was, 'I have known corpses to have stronger heartbeats than yours. It's so weak if you experience anything more exciting than a sudden change in the weather your heart would likely curse your stupidity and promptly decide enough is enough and explode.'"

Ebenezer looked at Butler. "It would be nice if occasionally you let one slip by."

"And give up one of my rare moments of fun? It's the only thing that gets me through the day, Sir."

"I'm ready Mr. Butler. Pass him down."

Butler handed Ebenezer to Lurch and climbed into the opening. He paused and stared over at the far side of the room. He thought he had detected a movement, a passing shadow. His gaze searched the darkness but found nothing that shouldn't be there. He climbed down and caught up with the others.

The assassin thief stepped out of the shadows, walked over to the trapdoor and listened to the sound of fading footsteps. When they had reached a safe distance, Shadow followed.

Furtive reached the end of the tunnel and paused at the steps leading up. His head lantern he directed aloft, highlighted the bottom of a trapdoor and the two iron bolts holding it firmly in place. He turned as the others arrived.

"Slide back the bolts and give it a shove with your shoulder," instructed Butler.

Furtive did as instructed but the trapdoor was heavier than he expected. He gave it a more forceful push. The soil, grass and weeds that had grown over it slid off when it swung open. Furtive poked his head above ground and looked at the ring of rocks surrounding the secret door. He climbed out and passed through a gap between the stones. Castle Drooge stood a couple of hundred yards distant. He turned and saw Drooge Manor a little closer. Lurch and Ebenezer joined him, Butler a few moments later. They all stared at the Manor as the sounds of pistols shots and breaking glass rang out.

"They are ruining your home, Sir," said Butler, sadly.

Ebenezer was unconcerned. "It's already a ruin. They can burn it to the ground for all I care. I'll buy a new one far from here when we find Jacobus's inheritance."

Furtive pointed at one of the figures striding purposefully for the manor. "There's Sabastian."

Ebenezer glanced at his brother and smiled. "I would have loved to have been there when he discovered his painting had been stolen and replaced with the one you painted, Butler."

"Yes, Sir, I was particularly proud of the lighting on your septic boil. It looked so real I often thought it might burst."

Ebenezer sniggered. "Ah, fun times, eh, Butler."

"Maybe now, Sir, that the image of your naked boil adorned bottom has begun to fade. I'm sure it's hard to decide which caused your brother the biggest shock, discovering his painting was missing, or setting eyes upon the one that had appeared."

"Maybe I'll ask him one day, but not today. We need to keep moving while Sebastian is distracted."

To the sound of gunshots, breaking glass and excited shouts of vandals smashing things, the four men rushed across the open ground toward the quarry.

Shadow had smiled on learning of Butler's masterpiece swapped for Sebastian's painting. Though a strange mix, they seemed like a fun crowd. It would be a shame if one or more of them had to die, but the life of an assassin-thief was not meant to be fun or filled with compassion. What must be done will be done swiftly and decisively, emotions would play no part. Shadow glanced at the manor, slipped from the top of the rock, landed silently on the ground and set off in pursuit.

They had almost reached the quarry entrance when Furtive glanced back. What he saw caused him to stop. The others joined him in staring at Drooge Manor and the flames in one of its upstairs windows.

Butler sighed. "There go my spare suits."

"And all that delicious brandy," said Furtive, sadly, but then smiled and tapped his pocket. "Though, of course, I did steal a couple of bottles for my own personal use." He pulled something from his pocket and smiling, held it out to Butler. "And I saved yer special limited-edition butler-themed toothbrush for yer."

Butler stared at the worn, grubby bristles pointing in every direction but upright and shivered in revulsion. "Please, keep it."

"Thanks, mate." Furtive stowed it in one of his seemingly bottomless pockets.

"A houseful of memories gone up in flames," commented Ebenezer, sadly.

Butler looked at Ebenezer in surprise. "Really, Sir, that's all you will miss?"

"What! Did I say that out loud? Bah! It's only a damn house. Bricks and mortar. Good riddance to it."

"That's better, Sir. You had me worried for a moment."

"As important as suits, brandy and memories are ter us all," said Furtive. "What about the two prisoners trapped inside?"

Butler stared at the window of the study. Though the shutters should prevent bullets from getting through, nothing would stop the flames once they took hold. "They'll be burnt to death! I'll have to go back and rescue them." He turned to Furtive. "You stay with Ebenezer and Lurch. I'll run back, set them free and meet you in the quarry."

Furtive nodded. "Don't worry about us."

"Would you like me to accompany you, Sir?" Lurch asked.

"Thanks for the offer, but you are needed here. Your job is to make sure no harm comes to Ebenezer."

"You can count on me, Sir."

Butler noticed the concerned expression of his employer. "You know it's the right thing to do, Sir. I can't be responsible for their deaths."

"I know, Butler, but please be careful. You get yourself killed and I absolutely will fire you this time."

"I know you will, Sir, and it will be deserved." Butler turned away and ran back across the moor.

The others watched him for a few moments.

"I suggest we keep moving, Ebenezer," said Furtive. "We are in the open here and if any of Sebastian's men spot us, they'll come and find out what we're doing."

"I agree, let's go."

They headed for the quarry.

"Do you think Mr. Butler will be okay, Sir?"

"I hope so, Lurch. I do hope so."

Shadow watched Butler sprint by and wondered why the man would risk his life to save those of his enemy. A glance toward the quarry revealed the three misfits going to find the treasure. Shadow had a decision to make.

Crakett Murdersin moaned as he stirred.

Because their chairs had been tied back to back to reduce their chance of escape before the others had fled, Milkwood had to look over his shoulder to see Crakett. "Are you awake, Mr. Murdersin?"

Crakett mumbled drowsily.

"Was that a yes?"

Crakett winced from the throbbing pain in his head, whose cause was not only from Butler's assault. "Don't you ever stop asking questions, Milkwood?"

"I'm sure I must do, but I am afraid this is not going to be one of those times. Though I know this might not be the best moment to bring this up, I was wondering about my fee?"

Crakett's gaze around the room took in every detail and object. "What about your fee?"

"Well, I was wondering when I was going to receive it?"

"Ignoring your atrocious performance in the scheme of things..."

"Oh, thank you, Sir. I knew you were a good sort and not one to let a little slip-up stop you from honouring our agreement."

"I will continue. ...in the scheme of things that have passed since you arrived here, my hands, in fact my whole body, is tied securely to a chair, so even if I was inclined to pay you your fee, it would be impossible for me to do so."

"I have a little movement in my arms, so if you could sort of squirm to the side a bit, I might be able to reach into the pocket where your money is secreted if you inform me which one that would be."

"If your hands go anywhere near my pockets it will be the last place they will go whilst still attached to your arms."

"Oh! Alright, Sir, you can pay me later, when you are free. Though I'm sure I don't know when that will be."

"In the next couple of minutes if all goes to plan."

"Is it a cunning plan, Sir? So cunning that if it was learnt of by a fox it would be so dismayed by its cunning slyness it would run toward the sound of hunters' horns and snarling hunting dogs and throw itself at them."

"No!"

"Oh! What sort of plan is it, then?"

"A simple plan."

"I'd prefer the plan to be cunning if there was a choice, Mr. Murdersin."

"Do you, Milkwood, have a cunning plan in mind?"

"Not right at this moment."

"Simple plan it is, then."

"Maybe you could add a bit of drama to your plan to make it less boring and then I think I could ignore its lack of cunning."

"I've never met anyone who likes the sound of his own nasally voice as much as you."

"Thank you, Mr. Murdersin."

"It wasn't a compliment."

"It was to me."

Crakett sighed. "I am sticking with my boring, simple plan and the first part is to manoeuvre our chairs around a bit, nearer the coffee table."

Arthur glanced over his left shoulder at the low table. "How do you expect us to do that?"

"Wiggle and throw your weight in the direction you want to move, which for you is toward the table, and I'll shove in the opposite direction, so we turn."

"I don't actually want to move. I'm quite happy here."

"If you don't move I'll rock these chairs back and forth so violently it will tip you over and your face will smash into the floor."

"It's always the threats with you. I've yet to hear a please or thank you pass from your lips."

Crakett rocked the chairs back and forth.

"Okay, okay! I'll help you with your unpretentious plan." In a lacklustre manner, Arthur attempted to edge the chair toward the coffee table. "It's no good, it's impossible. They won't move."

"My old, arthritic granny could do better than that," said Crakett. "And she's been dead ten years."

"Maybe you should go and fetch her then."

"Of all the people to be tied too, it had to be you."

"Yeah, well, you certainly would not have been my first choice either."

When a shot rang out and something struck the window shutter, Milkwood jerked his head at the loud impact. "What was that?"

"Either a particularly hard drop of rain, or a bullet," said Crakett.

"A bullet? Who would want to shoot at a house?"

"Probably someone who wasted money on a ticket for one of your plays, knows you are in here and wants payback."

"I'd have you know I received a standing..." Milkwood screamed when bullets peppered the shutter.

"Stop screaming like a girl, your hurting my ears. I doubt the bullets will penetrate through the shutter. We should be perfectly safe."

"That's alright for you to say. If a bullet gets in it will hit me first."

"It's true what they say; every cloud does have a silver lining. If you don't want to get shot, all you have to do is move your chair around a bit and we'll be free a few moments later."

More gun shots. More bullets struck the shutter. One got through, shattered the window and smashed a vase on the sideboard before burying itself in the wall.

Milkwood's attempt to move the chair a second time was a lot more enthusiastic.

"Stop!" Crakett ordered.

Milkwood breathed heavily as he stared at the bullet-holed shutter. "Are you sure? I can go farther."

"Any farther and we will have swapped positions."

"I see no downside to that."

"Rock from side to side to tip the chairs toward the table."

Milkwood glanced at the table and at the empty glass and the brandy decanter. "I see your plan; you will smash the glass or the decanter and use the sharp edges to cut through our ropes."

"Something like that," answered Murdersin, vaguely. "Now rock as if your life depended on it, which in fact it does."

The two captives rocked the chairs vigorously.

The chairs overbalanced and tipped. The top of the high backs struck one corner of the coffee table and flipped it into the air. Glass and decanter were catapulted skyward on higher trajectories and smashed into the crystal chandelier above them. The delicate teardrops of crystal forming the impressive chandelier split into slivers and fell. "Mr. Ebenezer won't like that," stated Milkwood. "That looked expensive and probably an antique or a family air loom." His worried eyes flicked across all the objects in play as the low table flipped completely over and came to a rest with one end on the sofa and the other resting on the edge of Crakett's chair seat. "I'm beginning to suspect this unpretentious plan of yours, Mr. Murdersin, is not as simple as you led me to believe."

The thicker glass and decanter suffered no damage by their collision with the delicate chandelier; the head the decanter plummeted toward would not be so lucky.

Milkwood watched the decanter fill his vision. Though it was not his first doubt that Crakett's simple plan might fail, it was the one that caused him the most concern. The decanter struck the side of his head before bouncing to the floor and he was concerned no more.

Crakett, unconcerned by the decanters trajectory, or in fact anything it struck during its downward plummet, stretched his head around to observe the falling shards of crystal. They tinkled onto the low table, slid down its angled length and dropped off the edge. Though most landed on the floor, a few fell into Crakett's open palm waiting to receive them. He selected the largest and a few swishes of the sharp edge sliced through his bindings. A few seconds later he was free. Without a glance at the unconscious actor, he brushed himself down and casually walked from the room.

Crakett ignored the bullets smashing through the glass of the front door and striking the carved woodwork and the peeling, mildewed papered walls. A glance up the stairs revealed the raging fire about to rip through the house. While Crakett contemplated his escape route, he turned toward the sound of approaching footsteps. His hand reached into the secret pocket of his jacket and pulled out his legendary fruit knife. His feet carried him silently into the shadows. His thirst for revenge bade him to wait.

Butler rushed through the wine cellar and leapt up the stairs three at a time. He entered the hall lit by flames creeping down the once magnificent stairs and hurried for the study. He never reached it. A jab to the throat from a slicing hand brought him to an air gasping halt. He froze when a hand pulled his head back and a knife was pressed against his throat.

"Hello, Butler."

Though Butler recognized Crakett's voice, the knife held tight against his windpipe made it unwise for him to return the greeting.

"Where is the rest of your little gang?" Crakett released the knife pressure slightly.

"Gone," Butler replied a little hoarsely.

"Gone where?"

"Far away from this place by now. Sebastian's men turned up and we thought it wise to leave. I only came back because I noticed the fire and couldn't leave you and Arthur to burn. By the way, where is Arthur?"

"Where you left him, but slightly worse for wear."

"You killed him!"

Crakett shrugged. "Dead or alive, I have no concerns either way."

"You were going to leave him to burn."

"I have no desire for banter, only that you answer my questions, where are the paintings?"

"Ebenezer threw his on the fire and Sebastian's is in the garden, if his men haven't found it by now."

"If you are going to lie, at least say something convincing."

"If you don't believe me, look in the hearth in the dining room. I'm sure there's enough left of the painting to indicate I am telling the truth."

" It doesn't make sense that the old miser would burn it?"

"It does if you know what Ebenezer has been through. He is practically penniless; his grandfather's lost inheritance was to be his saviour. When we compared the two paintings we realized immediately it had all been a lie. A big joke played by Jacobus on his relations. There are no clues in the paintings and there is no hidden inheritance."

"How can you be so certain?"

"Because both paintings were identical down to the last brushstroke; that's why Ebenezer had me throw Sebastian's out the window and his into the flames. It went up in smoke like his dreams of a better life."

"I admit you tell a convincing story, but I still don't believe you."

"I told you where the proof can be found. Look or not, I am past caring. This whole fiasco has been nothing but a total waste of time."

"Why did you return Sebastian's painting?"

"It was Ebenezer's last shot at getting one over on his brother; he knew Sebastian would keep looking until the day he climbed into his grave. Ebenezer wanted him to continue wasting his time, forever hoping that one day all would become clear and the lost inheritance would at last be his."

Crakett thought for a few moments before dragging Butler into the dining room and over to the fireplace. He stared at the shrivelled, blistered canvas and the corner of the artwork that had survived the flames and sighed. "Though it seems you have told the truth, it won't save your life."

"I must admit it comes as no great surprise." Butler had slowly been moving a hand toward the pistol in his pocket. He stopped when he felt Crakett tense. *Had he guessed what I was trying to do?* He waited.

Crakett felt the gentle caress on his neck, a sudden pressure and then nothing. He was paralyzed from head to foot. His eyes, the only part of his body left with movement, looked to his left when something attracted his vision, a dark form. When he realized who it was he knew his death would not be long coming. He stared at the fabled assassin and watched as the mask was removed. If he had full control of his body, his eyebrows would have raised, and a shocked gasp would have escaped from his open mouth. Though his eyes did their best to display the man's astonishment, without the accompanying essentials to reinforce the astounded expression, it was as uninspiring as Arthur Milkwood's acting.

Shadow smiled.

Inside, Crakett screamed when fingers probed his neck until they picked out the required nerve points. He had heard of this death grip, it was called the *assassins caress.* He felt a gentle pressure on his skin and shortly after his heart ceased to beat.

Though Butler had no idea what Crakett was doing or where the scent of lilac that tickled his nostrils had come from, when he felt the man's knife arm slide limply down his sleeve, he grabbed the pistol from beneath his jacket and spun. Crakett flopped to the floor and lay still. Butler knelt and felt for the man's pulse, but didn't find it. Unsure what had killed the man so suddenly, but thought a heart attack most probable, he rushed from the room, entered the study and knelt beside Milkwood. A quick check proved him to still be alive. While he untied the rope, the man became conscious.

"Oooow, my head really hurts, Crakett."

Butler helped Milkwood to his feet. "Crakett's dead!"

Milkwood looked at his saviour in surprise. "Really?"

Butler nodded. "Yes, really. He's in the dining room. A heart attack I think."

"I don't suppose he happened to mention the fee I was promised before he died?"

"No, Arthur, he didn't. We have move quickly; upstairs is on fire and it won't be long before the whole house is aflame."

"In that case, lead the way my good man."

Butler rushed from the room and headed for the cellar. "There's a secret tunnel down here we can use to escape." He turned at the bottom of the steps to discover Milkwood's absence. He sighed and waited.

A loud crash in the hall reverberated through the ceiling. Milkwood appeared and shot a glance back along the hall. He grabbed the key from the hall-side lock, slammed shut the door and locked it. He smiled at Butler. "A plump man just smashed through the front door."

"Maybe he didn't notice the bell," quipped Butler, dryly. "You seem happier. I assume Crakett finally settled your account?"

Arthur nodded enthusiastically. "He has and also generously included a bonus for a job well done and a late payment charge he insisted I take."

"Strange, he didn't seem the generous sort to me." Butler headed for the secret door at the end of the wine cellar.

Milkwood smirked. "I believe it was death that changed him."

Butler grabbed the lantern he had left by the opening and led Milkwood down the steps.

"Crakett told me a little while ago," Milkwood continued, "that every cloud had a silver lining. Mine is obvious," he tapped the bulge in his jacket for emphasis, "but I bet he is finding it hard to find his now." Milkwood smiled. "It's a funny old life this acting lark."

Shadow followed them through the underground caverns.

16th
CHAPTER

FORCED ENTRY

Furtive, **Ebenezer and** Lurch stepped into the quarry's metal cage, which creaked in protest when it was forced to support the weight of the large man who had to stoop to fit inside. When Furtive released the ratchet that locked the cage in place, it descended faster than it had ever done before. The crash emitted when it struck the concrete base echoed through the quarry as the three men staggered out.

Furtive glanced at the slightly buckled cage. "On our return, Lurch, you will enter on yer own."

"Yes, Mr. Furtive, I agree. I don't think it was built to carry three passengers."

Furtive ignored the retort that sprung to mind and turned to Ebenezer. "Do yer know where Diablo's lair is?"

Ebenezer pointed into the quarry. "In the old gold mine near the far end."

Furtive pulled the four-barrelled blunderbuss out from under his coat and slapped it into a palm. "Then let's go and get yer inheritance Mr. Ebenezer."

Lurch lifted Ebenezer onto his back and followed the well-armed furtive thief.

Furtive's eyes searched the many darker patches for any sign of danger as he led them through the quarry. "Is this where the stone came from to construct the castle and yer manor, Ebenezer?"

"It is, though that was before my time."

"And the gold mine is what made your family wealthy?"

"Wealthier. Jacobus was already rich. He was a ruthless banker, a wise investor and a man who lived for making a profit by any means. People and acquaintances were mere tools to him, to be used and discarded when they had outlived their usefulness or no longer had funds."

"He sounds like a man who didn't make friends easily."

"He wasn't, though in the early days of his success he was different. He had friends then and even met a woman willing to put up with his stern outlook on life and business. As his wealth increased so did his despise of those around him. That's why he moved to this god-forsaken place where he could be alone and build himself a castle. When his wife's love turned to hatred, he had Drooge Manor built. She lived a practically solitude assistance until she died, alone and unloved. My father moved in when he returned from university and was groomed to take over the business."

"But why did Jacobus hide his wealth and not pass it on to his son, your father?"

"Because it was his and his alone. Even in death Jacobus couldn't tolerate even his own flesh and blood having it."

Furtive scrutinized the dark area shrouding a pile of large stones for a few moments before demising them as hiding no threat. "If Jacobus was so attached to his wealth, even in death, why did he commission the two paintings that held clues to its location?"

Ebenezer shrugged. "That, I am afraid, is a question I have often asked myself without arriving at any satisfactory answer. Perhaps he wanted his son, my father, to experience in part his own struggle for wealth, or perhaps he thought if my father was handed such a huge fortune he would shun the business empire he had taken so long to create and use the wealth to squander on a good and happy life. However, if that was the reason, it failed drastically; because my father spent a large part of his life obsessed with cracking the painting clues and ignored his father's businesses. Slowly but surely, Jacobus's empire began to crumble until only a small portion of Jacobus's empire remained profitable, which is now owned by Sebastian after he tricked me into taking businesses of no worth or heavily debt ridden when we shared out our father's inheritance them. He ruined me."

"That explains the rivalry between you."

"It was already firmly established long before that deceitful event. It was the reason my father left each of us a painting, in the hope we would reconcile, put the past behind us and become friends again. He wanted us to work together to solve the clues, which as you are now aware, failed miserably."

After a few moments silence, they rounded a turn and Ebenezer pointed at a dark opening in the night-shrouded rock face. "There's the goldmine."

Furtive stared at the ominous patch of darker black. "Diablo's lair!" He cocked Grave Filler and led his companions forward.

Though Sebastian had given the order for his men to fire a few shots at the house, he soon regretted the action when flames appeared in one of the upstairs rooms. If the paintings were inside, as he feared, they would be lost and with it his only hope of finding his grandfather's wealth. He had issued the order to cease fire and waited for his brother and his accomplices to rush from the house, hopefully with the two paintings in their possession, which he would promptly relieve them of. He had been waiting by the front door for a long time now and they still had not appeared.

Flint walked over and stood beside his grumpy employer. "I just checked with the men positioned around the house, Sabastian, and no one has come out yet."

Sebastian glanced at the upstairs windows when glass shattered from the heat of the flames ravaging the top floors of the house. "Break down the door. If they are still inside I want them, and my paintings, found and brought to me."

"Yes, Sir."

Flint ordered two men to help him and together they slammed their shoulders against the stout mahogany door, but it steadfastly refused to be forced open.

Rubbing a bruised shoulder, Flint approached Sebastian. "Sorry, the door is too strong. We'll need is a battering ram to get through it."

Sebastian glanced at each of the men around him and called him over with a beckoning wag of his finger.

The man, obviously a good eater if his plump form was any evidence, nervously stepped forward.

"What's your name?" Sebastian casually asked.

"Horace Arbuckle, Mr. Sebastian."

"Well, Horace, I want you to help me. We are going to show these men how to open that door."

Horace glanced at the solid door doubtfully. "If you say so, Sir. What do you want me to do?"

"First, give your weapon to Flint. Don't worry, you'll get it back in a minute."

Flint took the reluctantly offered weapon.

Sebastian moved to stand a short distance from the door and beckoned Horace to stand beside him. Sebastian looked at the door and then at Horace. "Let's move back one step."

They stepped back.

"Are you ready, Horace?"

Horace, believing they were going to rush the door and throw their weight against it, nodded he was.

"Good man, Horace. I will count down to three and then we act."

Horace nodded.

"Three."

Before *two* was spoken, Horace was fully aware of his employer's plan. He felt arms lift him off the ground and air rushing past from his flight toward the solid wooden barrier. The thump of his soft, but weighty, body striking the door was accompanied by his painful scream and the splintering of wood. He crashed through and rolled across the hall floor until he came to a halt with a crack of his head against the bottom step of the staircase. Slightly dazed, he looked back at the busted door hanging on its hinges and the smiling face of his employer peering through.

"Well done, Horace," praised Sebastian.

"Thank you, Sir," replied Horace, groggily.

Sebastian turned to Flint. "Search the house and don't come out unless you have the paintings."

"And if we can't find them, Sir?"

"Refer to my previous command for your answer."

Flint rallied his men and led them into the burning building.

Once inside, they glanced around the hall and the flames creeping down the staircase. Ceilings upstairs crashed to the floor.

"Forget about upstairs, split up and search down here, but hurry, we don't have long," Flint ordered.

The men spread out to search the ground floor.

Flint walked over to Horace and handed him back his weapon. "Are you okay?"

"I am, surprisingly. A few bruises and a sore head, but other than that I'm good."

"Stay in the hall and shout for everyone to get out if the flames start taking hold down here." Flint crossed the hall and entered the dining room. A search through the cupboards revealed nothing of interest. He glanced through the doorway when a loud crash reverberated through the house and a shower of sparks flew past the entrance.

Horace appeared with a terror in his eyes. "The ceilings and upstairs floors are collapsing. I think the house is about to cave in."

"Get the men out." Horace disappeared and his shouts for everyone to evacuate the building filled the house.

A crackling sound caused Flint to look up; the ceiling was awash with curling flames. When he crossed to the door, he happened to glance at the fireplace. He stopped and peered at something. He moved to the fireplace, knelt and stared at the shrivelled, burnt canvass. All except a small corner hanging over the edge of the grate turned to ash at his touch. He picked up the only piece to have survived and examined its details. Though Sebastian had briefly explained the features of his painting, it was difficult to tell if this was part of it. He stood, slipped the fragment in his pocket and turned toward the door. He halted when part of the ceiling collapsed and crashed to the floor. Forced back by the hot, acrid smoke and searing flames, Flint watched the smouldering lengths of timber that followed fall across the door, blocking his escape.

Flint rushed to the window, yanked it open and cursed when he saw the metal bars set into the frame. He turned, grabbed the end of the dining table that was not yet on fire and dragged it over to the window. He pushed it tight against the wall, climbed on top, laid on his back and kicked at the bars that refused to budge. He pulled out his pistol, aimed at the wooden frame where the metal bars slotted into the wood and fired. Splinters sprayed out. Two more shots left deep gouges in the frame. After he had repeated the process at the top of the bars, he lay on his back and kicked. The third blow sent the bars flying. The ceiling above him fell; Flint dived through the narrow gap and landed in the bush outside the window. Smoke, flames, sparks and pieces of burning timber followed in his wake.

Flint let out a sigh of relief, climbed to his feet and pushed through the undergrowth onto clear ground. He stared back at the house as internal walls and ceilings collapsed. He brushed the ash from his clothes, smoothed his hair back into place and headed for the front entrance. He halted after two steps and looked down at the painting one of his boots had ripped a big hole in..

Butler climbed out of the tunnel and looked back at the manor. The roof collapsed, shooting smoke, flames and sparks high into the night sky. Though the house had been old, damp, neglected and cold, it had been his home for twenty years: he mourned its loss.

Milkwood joined him. "There's no saving it now. Its destruction will only stop when there is nothing more for the flames to consume."

Butler turned away and sprinted for the quarry with Milkwood close behind. When they reached the road, Butler pointed at the railway bridge. "If you head that way until you reach the bridge and follow the railway line, it will take you to the nearest town. In the morning you can catch a train." He looked at Milkwood. "I suggest you never return here."

"You need have no fear of that. This is the worst acting part ever to come my way, and believe me, some have been terrible." He held out a hand. "I know we were on different sides in this affair, but if I had known the players before I wouldn't have been so keen to accept the role. Thank you for saving my life, Mr. Butler."

"If I said it was a pleasure, I'd be lying, but good luck, Arthur." Butler shook the man's hand and watched him walk away.

Milkwood turned and called out. "Let me know when you get a new address and I'll send some free tickets for my next play."

Butler raised an arm in thanks. The man would not be receiving his new address, of that he was never more certain. He moved over to the metal elevator and saw the cage below. He hoisted it up, climbed aboard and descended.

Flint slipped the painting off his foot and held it in the glow of the burning building. The details seemed to be some of those Sebastian had described from his painting. As he rolled it up, he imagined how pleased his employer would be when he handed him his painting back. Maybe he would get his bonus after all. Whistling a merry tune, he went to find his employer.

Sebastian, who stood near the road watching Drooge Manor burn, tried to ignore the annoying coughing and choking sounds discharged by the smoke seared lungs of the men around him. With the non-appearance of his brother and his companions, he assumed they had escaped through an exit unknown to him; probably a secret tunnel of some description. The collapsing roof sent out a whoosh of sparks, burning timber and a thick cloud of smoke that rolled across the neglected garden. A hazy form appeared in the smoke; a man. Sebastian watched the figure emerge. Beneath the layer of ash and smoke-blackened skin, he recognized Flint's ugly features. He hadn't perished in the burning house as he had thought. When he noticed Flint concealed something behind his back, he waited to find out what it could be.

"Hello, Sir."

Sebastian nodded. "Flint, you survived."

"Only just, Sir, but not all my pain and suffering were in vain and I believe, when you discover what I have found, you will be so pleased you will insist on thrusting a large bonus upon me."

"The only thing I will be thrusting in your direction if you don't get to the point is my dagger."

"Of course, Mr. Sebastian, I have some good news and some not so good news."

Sebastian glared.

"The not so good news is that I think I have found Ebenezer's painting."

Sebastian allowed the puzzled look of surprise to replace his impatient glare. "How can that possibly not be good news?"

"That, Sir, is, I fear, something you are about to discover." Flint pulled the singed painting fragment from his pocket and handed it to his employer.

Sebastian took it. "Ah! Now I see what you mean, nothing good is currently occupying my thoughts at this moment. I suppose the fire got to it before you could save it?"

"No, Sir, it had already been burnt before we arrived as I found it in Ebenezer's fireplace. That piece you hold was all that survived."

"Why would Ebenezer burn it?"

"I have no idea, Sir."

Sebastian looked at Flint. "I was thinking aloud."

"Sorry, Sir."

"What is the good news you have for me?"

"The good news, Sir, and my reason for mentioning my bonus a moment ago, is that I have found your painting and now have the honour of returning it to you." Flint revealed the rolled canvass previously concealed behind his back. Though it was hard to tell, and it could be his wishful thinking, he thought he saw the hint of a smile on his employer's lips.

Sebastian took the painting, unrolled it and held it up. If there had been a smile on his lips, it wasn't there now. Light from the burning building shone through the many bullet holes distributed about the canvass and through the large central L-shaped slit running almost the full width of the painting. The bottom flap of the rip flopped down to reveal Flint's smiling face.

Flint reached out a hand, gripped the drooping flap of canvas and held it back into position. "As you can see, Sir, with a minimum amount of restoration it will be as good as new."

"A minimum amount of restoration! It's more *hole* than canvas!"

"A slight exaggeration I think, Sir."

Sebastian threw the painting to the ground. "Even if it could be restored to its former glory, which it absolutely without a doubt cannot, what good is it when this is all I have of Ebenezer's?" He thrust the small scrap into Flint's face as emphasis. "Or are you going to tell me this can be restored as good as new also?"

"I think, Sir, that my expertise in art restoration has been ridiculed enough for one night, so I will decline to offer my opinion on the matter."

"Hallelujah. The man stops talking."

Sebastian noticed Flint stare off into the distance.

"Sir, do we have any men over by the quarry?"

Sebastian spun to face the quarry. "No, why?"

"I thought I saw someone."

Sebastian peered at the quarry entrance to the right of his castle, but saw no one. "Who did you see?"

Flint shrugged. "I'm not sure, Sir, it was only a fleeting glimpse, but it looked like that man of your brother's, the one who dresses like a waiter."

"Butler!" Sebastian smiled and glanced at the smoke stained man. "Well, Flint, it seems maybe not all is lost, and we might yet still salvage something from this disaster." He let the scrap of painting flutter from his hand.

"In this scenario, Sir, would my bonus also undergo a salvaging?"

"Let's not be too hasty, Flint. Round up the men and bring them to the quarry." Sebastian strode off with a long absent spring in his step.

Flint roused the men from their coughing and led them toward the quarry.

Figgins peeled off from the rear of the throng and ran across the weed-choked lawn. He picked up Sebastian's discarded painting and with a smile upon his lips, added it to his collection. *The wife will be pleased. Our house will look right posh like when I hang both paintings. The neighbours are going to be so jealous.* He let out a satisfied sigh and ran to catch up with the others. *Christmas couldn't get any better than this.*

However, as Figgins would soon find out, it could get a lot better.

17th
CHAPTER

LOST
INHERITANCE

With **the multi-barrelled** weapon held ready to dish out its deadly ammunition of buckshot, Furtive cautiously climbed the path that sloped up to the old mine entrance.

Lurch and his grumbling passenger followed a few steps behind.

They paused outside the dark opening while Furtive peeked around the edge of the rock to check if Diablo was at home. All he saw was the dark mineshaft leading deep into the rock. He stepped inside, increased the length of the flame in his head lantern and directed the brighter light around the tunnel. At intervals, stout timber supports and roof beams lined the hand-hewn tunnel. A large collection of animal bones, mostly sheep leg bones, Furtive thought, lay scattered on the ground. The burglar beckoned for Lurch and Ebenezer to come inside and whispered, "There's no sign of Diablo yet, so he might be deeper inside or not at home."

Ebenezer shot a glance behind. "If it's in the quarry it could sneak up on us. Put me down, Lurch. I'll walk in between you two."

Lurch gently lifted his master to the ground.

"As quiet as yer can, follow me." Furtive aimed the weapon along the tunnel and led them forward.

Diablo was very much at home. After its latest unappetizing meal of mutton, it had returned to its lair to rest its aching bones. It had soon fallen asleep and was currently having a very nice dream involving plump, succulent lambs, a leafy glade in a forest beside a gently babbling brook, and a very pretty female wolf named Blaze, so named because of the white streak of fur on her head, which he currently nuzzled. His nose twitched and much to his dismay, Blaze, the succulent lambs and the tranquil setting disappeared.

Diablo opened his eyes and raised his head to let his nose catch the sent that had woken him. He smelt something similar to mutton and something foul. It checked its paws, but they were clean. He looked toward the sound of approaching footsteps, moved into a crouch and hoping his back wouldn't fail him this time, prepared to spring as soon as the intruders were within range.

It was Furtive who spied Diablo first, not surprising really as he was in the lead and the only one of the three with a light. Though he had never set eyes upon the beast, he took it for granted the evil red eyes and wide-open mouth lined with teeth flying through the air toward him, did in fact belong to the satanic wolf he had been informed of. He raised Grave Filler and pulled the trigger. He felt himself knocked aside as the loud explosion filled the tunnel and heard the buckshot pepper the rock. He also heard Lurch's voice.

"Sorry, Mr. Furtive."

Furtive, wondering why the big man was sorry, bounced off the wall and slipped to the floor. He raised his head lantern toward the sound of vicious snarling and saw Lurch with his arms outstretched. Gripped in the man's large hands was the neck of the wolf.

Lurch, apparently unperturbed by the snarling lips and snapping jaws a few inches from his face, smiled at the devilish creature. He felt the wolf's warm breath; luckily a lot fresher smelling than Mr. Furtive's, wash over him. "Now, now, Wolfy," he said in a calm, soothing voice. "I know you are angry. I would be too if someone invaded my home, but we are not here to hurt you. We just want to pass by to go look for some treasure."

Diablo's snarls and snaps lessened. The wolf was puzzled. The voice was not one he was used to. He had been born in captivity and all he had known was cruelty and harsh words. This voice was different, soothing. The beast's natural instinct to attack and eat began to fade.

"That's better," soothed Lurch. "My, you are a big feller aren't you? Old as well by the look of your grey fur. Probably as old as my master as he has grey hair like you, but a lot less as you can see, more bald head than hair now."

As if he understood, Diablo glanced at the wrinkly human that smelled of mutton.

Ebenezer smiled nervously.

Furtive checked Grave Filler had not been damaged and climbed to his feet.

Diablo jerked his head around and snarled at the smelly human.

"Stay still Mr. Furtive," Lurch ordered.

Furtive froze.

"It's okay, boy, he won't hurt you. I am going to put you down, but I don't want you to attack anyone. I want you to be a good boy, okay?"

Diablo didn't answer, obviously.

Lurch placed the wolf on the ground and slowly released his grip. "Now that's better. You be a good boy and we can all be friends."

Sensing the big human posed him no threat, Diablo cocked his head to one side and stared at Lurch. He wanted to hear the voice again He had never heard anything like it before; it was so comforting and kind.

Lurch crouched before Diablo and held out his hand.

Diablo's eyes focused warily on the big hand reaching toward him and licked its lips.

Ebenezer half turned his head away, expecting the wolf to bite off the appetizing hand at any moment.

Furtive, who had the exact same concerns, placed a finger on the trigger and made ready to bring the weapon into use if the wolf attacked.

"It's okay, boy," said Lurch softly. "I'm not going to hurt you." He placed his large hand gently on the wolf's head and stroked. "That's nice, isn't it? I don't suppose anyone's ever stroked you or shown you any kindness before have they?"

Sadness appeared in Diablo's eyes.

Lurch moved a little closer.

Ebenezer gasped.

Lurch scratched behind one of the wolf's ears.

The wolf's eyes tried to look at the hand. It felt nice. It tilted its head to one side.

Lurch smiled. "Yes, I knew you'd like this." He moved his hand under Diablo's chin and scratched it gently.

Diablo purred like a giant kitten with a throat infection.

"You like that, don't you boy?" Lurch rubbed Diablo's side and when the wolf rolled onto his back, rubbed his belly.

Furtive relaxed the weapon. "I have never seen the like in all me life."

"He's always had a knack with animals," said Ebenezer. "I've seen birds land in his hand when he's holding food for them."

Ebenezer took a step nearer the wolf.

Diablo looked at him warily, but didn't snarl.

"It's alright, Mr. Ebenezer, come and say hello to Wolfy."

"Are you sure it's safe?"

"Yes, Sir, he's like a big puppy."

Ebenezer looked at Diablo's teeth. Puppy certainly didn't spring to mind. To play it safe he moved around Lurch and nervously touched the wolf's back. Gaining courage when nothing was bitten off, he stroked and scratched the wolf's back. "He likes it," said Ebenezer, hardly believing he was stroking the feared Diablo.

"I don't think he's been shown much kindness, Sir." It was said in a tone that hinted he had once suffered a similar experience. "But he will now."

Ebenezer used both hands to lavish attention on the wolf. "It's quite therapeutic actually. Just what the doctor ordered. He said I should get a pet."

"Um, no, Sir. If I recall, the doctor said, 'You should find yourself a companion, a live-in nurse to look after you and you should stay away from animals because...'"

"Butler!" Ebenezer stood up and gazed at his friend with a concerned expression. "Is everything okay?"

"Yes, Sir, everything is fine. Crakett is dead; he had a heart attack I think. Arthur has gone to the train station, fully paid, and your house is all but destroyed."

"I don't care about the rest, it's you I'm worried about, are you sure you are all right?"

"Yes, Sir, I am good, I promise."

"What about Sebastian and his men?" inquired Furtive.

"They were watching the house burn last time I saw them." Butler looked at the wolf licking Lurch's face. "I see Lurch has tamed the devil."

"I wouldn't 'ave thought it possible if I had not witnessed it with me own eyes," said an amazed Furtive. "A minute ago, it was a snarling, ferocious beast preparing to rip us to shreds, and now it looks no more frightening than a kitten."

"Can you control it, Lurch?"

"Yes, Mr. Butler. He'll be alright now he knows we are his friends."

Butler glanced along the tunnel. "I assume if your grandfather's inheritance is down here, it lies in that direction."

Ebenezer nodded. "It does."

"Furtive, would you like to lead the way?"

"I'd be glad to."

"Can you walk, Sir?"

"Of course I can walk. I may be old, riddled with boils, bunions and many other ailments, some never before known to man, and have one foot firmly in the grave, but when there is a great treasure to be had I could climb a mountain."

"Maybe a very small one, Sir, a gently sloping hill perhaps," said Butler.

Furtive led the way with Ebenezer and Butler behind him. Lurch and his new-found friend, Wolfy, followed at the rear.

Shadow, who had followed them inside and witnessed Lurch, amazingly, befriend the wolf, watched the unlikely group of friends head deeper into the mine and felt a little jealous of their close companionship. *It must be nice to have friends.*

Making the decision to let them keep their treasure, Shadow turned and walked away.

It took them ten minutes to reach the barrier in the form of a brick wall that stretched the height and width of the passage.

Ebenezer walked up to the wall and laid a hand upon it. "The treasure must be behind this."

Butler looked at Lurch. "What do you think; can you knock a hole through it?"

Lurch walked up to the wall and tapped it with his knuckles "I think so, Sir." Lurch turned to Diablo. "Wolfy, sit!"

Diablo obeyed and sat with his tongue lolling out, his gaze rarely moving from his new master.

Lurch moved to the middle of the wall and kicked it with the sole of his foot. A dull thud echoed through the mine. The joints around the area of impact cracked. A second kick curved in a section of wall. The third kick produced a large hole.

When the bricks had stopped falling and the dust settled, Butler shone his lantern into the hole and stepped through. The others followed and joined Butler in looking around the large metal vault constructed from sheets of riveted iron. Though a little rusty, it still seemed in good shape. Ebenezer crossed to the large door set in the front and pointed at the combination dial. "Damn, we need a code to open it."

Furtive flexed his fingers with a loud crack of knuckles. "A code isn't necessary when you have the service of the world's greatest burglar."

"You think you can crack it?" Butler asked.

"Of course. I am the best safe-cracker there is."

"Excuse me for doubting your skills, but how do you know you are the best safe-cracker in the world?" asked Ebenezer. "Do you thieves have an annual competition or something to determine who is the best?"

"Well, no, not exactly, I just sort of know I am," said Furtive.

"I'm not knocking your skills or anything, I was just interested, that's all," Ebenezer explained.

Furtive approached the safe and examined the dial.

"So, if I understood correctly, your skill level compared to all the other safe-crackers in the world is one you've set yourself."

Furtive glared at him. "I need absolute quiet or I can't do this."

Ebenezer nodded.

Furtive put his ear to the door beside the dial.

"It's just that Butler could say he is the best butler in the world, but that doesn't mean he is."

"Oh, but Sir, I think you'll find I am."

Ebenezer looked at Butler. "Would that be another self-appointed title?"

Butler thought about it for a few moments. "Best we keep quiet, Sir, so Furtive can do his job."

Furtive spun the dial to the right until he heard a faint click. He turned it to the left. Click! He continued and following the fifth click the rasping of metal from within the cavity of the door signalled the mechanism to unlock the vault had been activated. "That should be it."

Butler had noticed the code that unlocked the safe. "The combination was your grandfather's date of birth and death and the age he died," he told Ebenezer. "18, 17, 18, 88, and 71.

"Damn my foolishness," said Ebenezer. "That's why he included an image of himself in the paintings; it was a clue."

Furtive coughed to attract their attention. "Would you like me to open it?"

Excited by what they were about to see, Ebenezer nodded enthusiastically.

Furtive spun the four-handled wheel and one by one the thick bolts around the door were heard retracting. He pulled on the long lever to release the final catch and the door swung open. A stream of musty air tainted with decay whooshed out. All gazed through the opening and all were astonished by what they saw inside. Jacobus Drooge!

"Now of all the things I imagined concealed behind that door," said Furtive. "That was not one of them."

They entered and stared at the decayed skeletal corpse of Ebenezer's grandfather sitting proudly in a large ornate chair inlaid with golden details. His expensive hand tailored suit still possessed an air of elegant style. The white shirt, yellowed with age, not so much. Even in grisly death his persona was of a man of wealth.

The taught skin stretched over boney hands and skull had browned to the colour of ancient parchment. The sunken eyes stared but did not see. Lips pulled back in a gruesome grin, smiled at them, whether in a mocking or congratulatory manner for finding his inheritance, was unknown. What was known by all present was that it was awfully creepy.

Diablo walked up to the ghastly corpse and gave it a sniff. He visibly shuddered. It was the worst mutton he had ever encountered and declined taking a bite.

"One would hope he looked more handsome when he was alive," said Ebenezer.

Butler noticed Furtive's eyes focused hungrily upon the large jewel encrusted ring on one of the dead man's boney digits. "Just to let you know, Furtive, I will check the ring is still there before we leave."

Furtive huffed in an insulted manner. "I'm a lot of things, but I won't rob from the dead."

Butler raised an eyebrow in argument.

"Well, okay then, I would," Furtive conceded, "but not now you've noticed it I won't."

The three men and the wolf turned their attention to the other less creepy objects in the vault and all—except for Diablo who didn't really care unless it was edible and preferably not mutton—were a little disappointed by what they saw; three wooden crates one yard long and half that wide and high.

"Hmmm," uttered Butler.

"I thought there would be more, especially after seeing the size of this vault," stated Ebenezer, his disappointment impossible to miss.

"How about we open them before contemplating suicide," suggested Furtive. "Just 'cause it's only three small crates don't mean they ain't full of valuable stuff."

With tail wagging, Diablo wandered over to the crates. When he had stiffed each in turn and discovered none contained anything he could eat, he was also disappointed.

Butler pointed at the nearest crate. "Lurch, can you please open it."

Lurch moved to the nearest crate, gripped the lid and with a loud screech of nails being pulled from the wood, ripped it free.

It was full to the brim with neatly stacked wads of one-thousand-pound bank notes.

"See, I told yer," stated Furtive. "There has to be a million pounds in that one at least. If the others contain the same as this one, that's..." He paused to count on his fingers. "...a flipping lot of cash."

Ebenezer pulled a wad out sucked their scent into his hairy nostrils as he flicked through them. "I love the smell of money, even if it is a bit musty." He glanced at the other two crates. "I wonder if they do all contain the same."

"Let's find out, shall we, Sir," said Butler. "Lurch, the next one please."

Lurch leaned the nail studded lid he still held against the back wall of the vault and effortlessly ripped free the next one.

Bathed in the yellow glow that radiated from the crate, they stared at the gold ingots stacked neatly inside.

Ebenezer, close to tears of joy, fell to his knees and, with a certain amount of heaving and struggling, lifted out one of the bars. "It's so beautiful."

Furtive could also not resist picking one up. "I can't even imagine what all this is worth, but I know summink, we're rich, filthy stinking rich."

Ebenezer glared at Furtive. "Correction, Furtive, I am the one who's rich, your just filthy stinking a bit less poor than you were before, when I pay you."

"Of course, Sir, I apologize. The sight of the gold made me all excited. I even forgot to mention me bonus like I said I would."

"So excited it seems," said Ebenezer, "that it made you drop that bar of gold you held but a moment ago straight into your pocket."

Furtive looked at his empty hands in mock surprise. "Oh, golly gosh, thank yer for pointing that out. I hadn't noticed. It must have slipped from me hands" He reluctantly fished the gold bar from his pocket and placed in back in the crate.

Ebenezer returned his to the empty slot. "Lurch, I think it's best you replace the lid to avoid any more such mishaps."

"Yes, Sir." Lurch squeezed past Furtive who seemed reluctant to move away from the gold, laid the lid in place and hammered in the nails with his fist."

They turned their attention to the remaining unopened crate. "So far there's been bank notes and gold, each more valuable that the one before," said Butler, "so if the theme continues, this one has to contain something really special."

Ebenezer gazed at the crate. "I'd be happy if was another one filled with gold. Lurch, do your thing."

Lurch pried open the crate with his fingers.

The lantern light shimmered off the facetted diamonds that filled the crate. Some were large, and others were not so large, but none they saw could be said to be small.

All were speechless.

Butler land a hand on Ebenezer's boney shoulder. "Well, Sir, it seems your money troubles are well and truly over."

Ebenezer scooped out a handful of the precious stones and let them dribble back into the crate. "They certainly are."

"Mr. Ebenezer, Sir, when it comes to the time yer pay me, I wouldn't mind if a few diamonds were included."

Ebenezer looked at Furtive. "You are in luck, Furtive; you have caught me in a good mood. You have performed excellently during this venture and I am quite certain without your help we would not be here now."

"I agree wholeheartedly," said Butler.

"So," continued Ebenezer, "I think it's only fair that we forget about our original contract and pay you a fair amount for services rendered. To this end, how would you like to be paid fully in diamonds and a wad of bank notes for your immediate expenses?"

Furtive beamed. "I would like that very much, Sir."

"Hold out your hands."

Furtive's hands shot out to form as large a palm bowl as he could.

Ebenezer filled them to overflowing with the precious stones.

Furtive poured them into his pocket without spilling a single gem. "Thank you, Ebenezer."

"No, thank you, Furtive, and you can keep that gold bar you slipped in your pocket a moment ago when Lurch brushed past you to seal the crate."

"Thank you, Sir. Sorry, I can't help it. It's my nature."

Ebenezer grinned. "I know, Furtive, you are a thief and always will be I expect."

Butler helped Ebenezer to his feet.

"Lurch, seal the crates and then we'll think about how we get them out of here."

Ebenezer grabbed a thick wad of bank notes and handed them to Furtive, who promptly caused them to disappear into one of his capacious pockets.

Butler turned his thoughts to moving the precious cargo. "If Lurch can carry the gold crate, Furtive and I should be able to drag the other two out of the quarry."

"I have some rope we can tie around them to make them easier to move," said Furtive.

Butler nodded. "I was relying on that."

Furtive fished out two coils of rope and set about securing them around the crates.

"What are we going to do when we get up top?" Ebenezer asked. "We can hardly drag these along the road. My brother or his men would see us for sure."

"I admit it is a problem, Sir. Perhaps we can hide somewhere until Sebastian and his men have gone. The stables are far enough away from the house to escape the flames, so when the coast is clear I can nip to the stable, hitch the horses up to the carriage and load the crates. We can then head far away from here."

"It might work," said Ebenezer. "As a temporary measure we can head for Havasham Hall; Agnes will give us a bed for the night. In the morning we can make plans about what to do next, but I doubt my brother believes we perished in the fire. He'll suspect we used an escape route and might at this very moment be looking for us."

"Maybe we should leave the treasure here, Sir, until we are certain it's safe to move."

"I am not leaving the inheritance behind, Butler. It's taken me too many years to find."

"It's what I thought, Sir." Butler took the rope tied to the diamond crate Furtive held out.

Lurch picked up the crate of gold like it weighed no more than a sack of potatoes.

Butler was continually astonished by the man's strength. "Not too heavy, Lurch?"

"No, Sir, it's fine."

Ebenezer approached his grandfather, placed a boney hand on one not too dissimilar and said softly, "Thank you, Jacobus." He gave the dead man a slight nod, turned away and exited the vault.

As Butler watched the others leave, he noticed Furtive glance longingly at Jacobus Drooge's large ring before he stepped out, dragging the money crate behind him. Butler looked at the corpse's face. "I hope this has all been worth it, Jacobus." he said quietly. He gripped the rope and pulled the crate of diamonds out of the vault.

To seal his grandfather in his chosen tomb, Ebenezer attempted to shut the door, but it was too heavy. "Give me a hand Lurch."

Lurch stepped up to the door and, because his arms held the crate of gold, shoved it with a shoulder. The sound of the door slamming shut echoed through the mine. From within the vault came the sound of something ancient and bony crashing to the floor. Something, which seemed roundish in shape, rolled across the floor and struck the door with a dull thud.

Lurch looked at his master and shrugged. "Sorry, Sir."

"I guess it's not so much *rest in peace* as *rest in pieces*, for old Jacobus, now," joked Furtive.

Ebenezer shook his head to show his dismay, turned the handle to lock the door and spun the combination dial.

"Sir, you go first, then Lurch, Furtive and me at the rear. The wolf can go where it likes."

They headed for the mine entrance a lot richer than when they entered.

Butler and Furtive were panting from the strain of pulling the crates by the time they reached the quarry exit.

Butler dropped the rope and glanced at the top of the wall. "I'll go up first to check all is clear. If it is, I'll lower the cage. Send up the gold first with Ebenezer, as he is the lightest, then Furtive and his crate and then you Lurch, with the last one."

Everyone except Lurch nodded their agreement.

"What about Wolfy?"

"What do you mean?" asked Butler, glancing at the wolf.

"We can't leave him behind now we're all such good friends." Lurch pleaded.

Butler glanced at Ebenezer, who shrugged in a non-committal manner.

"I suppose if you want to keep him, Lurch, bring him up with you."

"I do, Sir, and I will. Thank you, Sir." He bent down to stroke his new pet.

Though it had no idea why, Wolfy wagged its tail excitedly.

Butler hoisted the cage to the top and stepped out. A glance at the distant manor revealed a large pile of smoking stone and smouldering timber. Only one end wall remained standing to hint at what had been there before. When something prodded the small of his back, Butler twisted his head. One of Sebastian's men held the pistol that had recently made its presence known.

Sebastian appeared out of the shadows with the rest of his armed men and smiled in a satisfied manner. "Hello, Butler."

"Hello, Sebastian! Are you out for a pleasant evening stroll?"

"I've yet to note anything pleasant about this evening so far, but I am hoping that is about to change. Did you find anything interesting down in the quarry?"

Butler shook his head casually. "Not anything you would be interested in."

"That is something I will decided that for myself." He glanced at the armed man covering the manservant. If he tries to escape, shoot him." Sebastian walked to the edge of the wall and gazed down. "Hello, brother."

Ebenezer gazed up. "Sebastian!"

"We have Butler held at gunpoint, so do exactly as I say, or you know what will happen." Sebastian's eyes flicked greedily over the wooden boxes below. I assume that's my inheritance in those crates."

"No, this is mine. I solved the clues and found it," argued Ebenezer.

"A mere technicality I aim to ignore totally. Send up the crates and no one will be harmed."

"I'd rather die than let you have it," Ebenezer spat.

"If that is your wish, brother, it can easily be arranged, however, others might also get hurt in the process." He waved some of the men forward and they aimed their weapons at those below.

Realizing he had no choice, Ebenezer reluctantly conceded. "Okay, Sebastian, you win. I'll send them up."

"I'll be waiting." He turned to one of his men. "Lower the cage and bring it up when the crates are aboard."

"Yes, Sir." Jekyll went to carry out his orders.

Sebastian returned to the wall. "I must congratulate you on your efforts tonight, brother, you surprised me. Especially how you managed to make me believe the hunchback was working for me when he was all the time your man. Very clever."

"You are an idiot, Sebastian. He *was* working for you, though not as you planned. He came to my house to steal my painting."

"You are lying, he was at the castle, supposedly guarding my painting, but he stole it instead."

"That wasn't Crakett, that was my man, Furtive, posing as Crakett. It was he who stole your painting."

A little taken aback, Sebastian hid his surprise. "Even more impressive. So where is the real Crakett Murdersin?"

"Dead!"

Sebastian shrugged and smiled. "This night just keeps getting better. One less man to pay. Two if you count Shadow."

"Why, what happened to Shadow, whoever that is?" Ebenezer asked.

"Come now, Shadow was also working for you."

"Wrong again, brother. I've had no communication with this Shadow or laid eyes upon him."

"It matters not. Hopefully he was in the house when it went up in flames. Dead or alive, he's getting nothing from me."

A short distance away, Shadow narrowed her eyes and glared at Sebastian.

Eager to see what was inside and how rich he had become, Sebastian excitedly watched Lurch load the first crate into the cage.

"You have a fine bunch of men, Sebastian."

Sebastian glanced at his men and then at Butler. "They have their moments," he muttered disinterestedly.

"They couldn't have been cheap, fine men like this."

"Cheap enough," Sebastian mumbled.

Butler spoke to nearest man who aimed a pistol at his chest. "Now you, Sir, must be earning at least twenty pounds a day for work like this."

"Twenty!" scoffed Maggot. "I'd be so lucky."

"Oh," uttered Butler with feigned surprise. "Fifteen then?"

The man, somewhat disheartened, shook his head.

"Not ten, surely?"

The man, a little embarrassed, held up seven fingers, "Eight is what he pays us."

"That's less the minimum going rate for a thug of your caliber." Butler shook his head disapprovingly. "Eight pounds! I've never heard the like, and on Christmas Eve. Perhaps you have been promised a large Christmas bonus to make up for such a miserly wage, is that it?"

Maggot sheepishly shook his head. "Not exactly, no."

Sebastian glared at Butler. "Stop it!"

Flint approached Butler. "Just out of interest, like, what's the going rate for the man in charge of this sort of operation?"

"With this many men under his control and working Christmas eve, minimum would be forty pounds a day, but I would expect him to be getting more."

"Forty! Not twenty then?"

Ben Hammott

"For all that responsibility, of course not. Your men should be getting at least twenty a day each."

"Shut up. Butler!" warned Sebastian, sternly.

"Nah, it's okay, I wanna hear what he has to say," said Flint.

Shadow smiled, let the knife slip back into its sheaf and, with a certain amount of amusement, watched Butler's cunning tongue cause chaos in Sebastian's ranks.

"Ebenezer pays more does he?" enquired Flint.

"Of course, even though he's a miser like his brother, he knows the true value of those who work for him. I tell you, if you men had done such a good job such as you have tonight under his employment, with bonuses you would receive one thousand pounds each, two of course for you as the man in charge."

A shocked gasp of surprise rippled through Sebastian's men.

"A thousand pounds," gasped Maggot."

Sebastian approached Butler in a threatening manner. "I said, shut up!"

Flint pointed his pistol at his employer. "Let's not be too hasty, *Sir.*"

Sebastian froze and sighed.

Butler grinned. *His plan was working.* "In fact, Flint, if you and your men would opt to switch sides, Mr. Ebenezer will pay each of you right now, *in cash*, a thousand pounds, two for you, and then you can go home and join your families and be with them when they wake on Christmas day."

"I'll match his offer and raise it by ten pounds," countered Sebastian reluctantly.

Butler noticed the faltering indecision on Flint's face. "Look, Flint, you don't know me, but you know Sebastian, a man, who if he told me the sky was blue and the grass was green, I would nip outside to check. I am a worker like you and your men. I assure you I am a man you can trust and so is Ebenezer. I will not barter, I have said what each of you will be paid and I stand by that. It is up to you and your men to decide which of us you trust to actually give you the wage you deserve." He turned to Maggot and shook his head. "Eight pounds."

The men started talking amongst themselves. It was obvious a few moments later when they fell to silence and diverted their weapons at their previous employer, exactly whose offer they had decided to accept.

Flint though kept his weapon trained on Butler. "Alright, Butler, we've made our choice, but until we get paid my gun stays aimed at you."

"You can't do this, Flint. We had an agreement. I'll pay you twice what Butler offered."

"Words from your mouth, Sebastian, are worthless, me and my men ain't, so shut up or face the consequences." He glanced at his men. "If he talks or moves, shoot his kneecaps."

The sound of weapons being cocked spread through the men.

"I'll need to talk with Ebenezer to arrange your payment."

Flint motioned at the wall with the weapon.

Butler walked over and peered into the quarry. "Hello, Sir."

Ebenezer gazed up at the voice. "Butler, what's going on up there?"

"I'll explain in a minute, Sir, but first I need you to send up..." He looked at Flint. "How many men do you have?"

"Fourteen, plus me."

Butler looked back at Ebenezer. "...Sixteen thousand pounds."

"Sixteen thousand pounds! Whatever for?"

"Please, Sir, I'll explain in a minute. I also need some rope. Furtive will have some, I'm sure."

"Will this do, Butler?"

Butler turned to see Furtive sitting on the wall with a glass of brandy in one hand and a lit cigar in the other, which also held a coil of rope.

Astonished by the man's sudden appearance, Flint asked, "Where did you come from?"

Furtive shrugged. "Somewhere and nowhere."

Flint had no idea what that meant.

Butler took the rope and passed it to Flint. "Your money is on the way." He pointed to the single tree that had not seen a leaf on its dead branches for a very long time. "Have one of your men tie Sebastian to that tree so he is facing the manor he burnt down."

Flint handed the rope to the nearest man, who had heard Butler's instructions and with the help of two others dragging their ex-employer, eagerly set off to complete the task.

Flint sniffed the air and checked his shoes.

"Okay, pull it up," called out Ebenezer.

The man at the hoist raised the cage.

Ebenezer stepped off a few moments later, shot a surprised glance at the bound form of his brother and then handed the banknotes to Butler. "What's going on?"

"In a minute, Sir." Butler handed the money to Flint, who promptly counted it, took out two of the high value banknotes for himself and passed the others around. When all had been paid he held out a hand. "Well, Butler, it's been a queer old night it has and I'm glad it's finally done with."

Butler shook the man's hand. "I know exactly what you mean."

Flint cocked his head at his former employer. "You okay with sorting him out?"

"Yes, Ebenezer and I will handle Sebastian."

"Okay, we'll be off. Some of us have a fair way to travel and there's a train due soon me and the men would like to be on. Merry Christmas, Butler, and thanks."

"Same to you, Flint, and Flint, I don't expect you or the men to ever return to Sebastian's employment."

"No need to fret about that. If I never set eyes on the man again it will be a day too soon and I'm certain the men are of a like mind." He doffed his hat to Ebenezer. "Merry Christmas, Mr. Drooge and sorry about yer house." He moved off and caught up with the men already walking off along the road. All were examining their thousand-pound banknotes, which until a few moments ago, had been nothing more than a myth.

"I tell yer, Butler," said Furtive. "With those sweet, tricky, persuasive words of yours, I don't think there's any situation yer couldn't talk yer way out of."

"You turned my brother's men against him," said Ebenezer, astonished.

"Yes, Sir, it wasn't hard. Your brother is not as considerate an employer as you. He's probably been berating them all night and, of course, the money was a huge incentive. However, we still have one problem left to sort out." Butler nodded to the man tied to the tree.

Ebenezer glanced over at his brother. "I'll have a talk with him."

"And I'll have Lurch send the crates up, Sir." Butler went to talk to Lurch.

Ebenezer went to talk to Sebastian.

Furtive drunk brandy and blew pungent smoke rings into the sky that swirled around the snow that had begun to fall in thicker clumps. It was going to be a white Christmas. Furtive sighed contentedly.

Ebenezer stood before his brother. "For once you are very quiet. No threats of malice or revenge. That's not like you, Sebastian. Could it be you have finally accepted your defeat?"

Sebastian shrugged, which didn't really work that well due to him being securely tied to the tree. "To tell you the truth, Ebenezer..."

"That'll be a novelty."

"...I'm fed up with the whole thing and I'm glad it's over. Yes, obviously, I would have preferred our positions were reversed, but I have money, I won't starve. Perhaps after all that's happened between us it's only fair you end up with the spoils."

Ebenezer stared at his brother with deep suspicion. "Forgive me if I don't believe a word that sprouts from your deceitful lips, but you needn't worry, you'll get your fair share of grandfather's inheritance."

Sebastian looked at his brother in shocked surprise. "After all I've done to you, you are still going to share it with me? You know I would not have done if our roles were reversed."

"It is something I'm well aware of. Look at me, Sebastian, I am old, weary and not much longer for this world. There is far too much wealth for me to spend in the time I have left or even if I lived two lifetimes, so why shouldn't I share?"

With regret masking his features, Sebastian said, "We have wasted much of our lives hating each other when we should have not. I misjudged you, Ebenezer, and I am sorry. I don't expect your forgiveness..."

"That's just as well because I won't be giving it, ever! What you did to Nancy can never be forgiven."

"That is the trouble with you, Ebenezer, you dwell in the past instead of living for the future."

"A future you took from me and poor Nancy."

"If I could change what happened, perhaps I might, but I can't. It happened and there's nothing we can do about it."

"You are not a good man, Sebastian. You need to change before it's too late, though I fear that time has long passed you by. You reap what you sow, and you have been reaping all your life. When the time comes your punishment will not be swift or pleasant."

"I am ready to receive whatever comes my way. I will not apologize for the way I have spent my life to you or God on high."

"I pity you, Sebastian, but I cannot save you, no one can."

Diablo bounded over, nudged Ebenezer playfully and growled at Sebastian.

"Is that, Diablo!"

"No," said Lurch, looking over. "This is Wolfy, and he's my friend."

"You are welcome to him," said Sebastian eyeing the large beast fearfully until it bounded off toward Lurch. "I assume with the wolf's appearance, it was hidden in the old mine all this time?"

Ebenezer nodded. "So close, right under your nose in fact."

"I'm going to fetch the horse and carriage, Sir."

"Okay, Butler."

"What, that old thing of yours," Sebastian scoffed. "You'll be lucky to get past the bridge with all of you and the treasure aboard, take mine. It's in the courtyard and the horses are still hitched. When I was in possession of both paintings, I planned to go somewhere quiet to study them."

Ebenezer stared at his brother suspiciously.

"He's right, Sir. Your carriage is rather old and small for all of us and the crates."

Ebenezer nodded his agreement.

The two brothers watched Butler head toward the castle.

"You have a good man there, Ebenezer. He is loyal to you."

"I know. I'd be lost without him."

Twenty minutes later, the crates were on board Sebastian's larger and much sturdier carriage. Furtive sat inside to protect the valuable cargo from thieves and Lurch and Wolfy sat beside Furtive to protect the valuable cargo from him.

Ebenezer and Butler approached Sebastian.

Ebenezer tipped a large handful of diamonds into his brother's pocket and Butler slid a thick wad of banknotes under the man's jacket.

The sharing out of the spoils seems to be a bit one sided," said Sebastian.

"Just as it was when you divided up our father's estate. Yet even that which you have been given is more than you deserve, and don't forget, I have to buy a new home now because of you."

Sebastian looked at Ebenezer. "So, brother, what happens now?"

Butler fiddled with the rope knots behind the tree.

"We will leave you to your gloomy castle to which I will never return. I hope you find a way to enjoy the rest of your miserable life, brother." Ebenezer turned away.

"But you can't leave me tied up like this. I'll freeze to death."

Butler stepped in front of Sebastian. "I have loosened the knots; a little struggling will set you free." Butler turned to glance at the manor when a crash rang out. Sparks and fresh flames reached into the sky. The final wall had collapsed. He turned back to the bound man. "I hope this is at an end, now, Sabastian. You have caused your brother enough pain and misery over the years, so let him live the rest of his life in peace." He leaned close to Sebastian's face. "If you have any thoughts of revenge, I suggest you here and now suppress them, because if you come after Ebenezer or the inheritance, I will kill you." Butler turned and walked away.

Butler helped Ebenezer into the carriage, wrapped a blanket around him and climbed up onto the front. After brushing the accumulated snow from the driver's seat, Butler sat, flicked the reigns and guided the horses along the track.

Ebenezer stuck his head out of the window and looked at Sebastian. "Merry Christmas, brother."

Sebastian scowled and while he struggled to free himself from his bonds, he watched the falling snow claim them from his sight.

Butler glimpsed dawn breaking on the horizon between gaps in the falling snow and sighed. It was the start of a brand-new day for them all.

18th
CHAPTER

UNEXPECTED
ARRIVALS

Snow **coated the** landscape in its picturesque coat of white, making even the dreariest, ugliest landscape one a pleasure to behold. Even a dung-pile or garbage heap was transformed into a white sculpture that belied the eyesore that lay beneath.

Leaving behind a trail of hoof-prints that stretched as far as the eye could see, the horse galloped along the track at breakneck speed. Salty sweat formed on its flanks and its nostrils flared to expel two streams of hot breath brought forth by the forced exertion its rider insisted upon.

The rider, unconcerned for the animal's welfare, urged the horse up the steep incline and on reaching the top spied the reason for his hurried dash. The rider glanced down at the town spread out at the bottom of the snow-blanketed hill, dotted with shrubs and bushes whose twigs and branches sagged under the weight of their cold, white loads. A few lights in some of the small houses signalled its inhabitants were beginning to awake and would soon be enacting in the festivities Christmas Day decreed. The rider had no time for such frivolities; all were a waste of time, effort and money.

The rider directed his gaze upon the carriage it was quickly gaining upon.

When the horse drew closer, the rider noticed the thick velvet curtains drawn across the carriage windows to keep the chill weather and gave the rider's plan an even greater chance of success. The rider steered the horse alongside the moving carriage, matched its speed, stood on the saddle and deftly stepped from the horse to the carriage.

The horse, glad to be free of its cruel master, slowed and for a moment watched the carriage drive away. It turned its head to look at the town before turning around and heading back the way it had come.

The intruder on the carriage climbed onto the top, drew a sharp dagger from its sheath and crept toward the unsuspecting driver.

Butler, unaware that death approached, blew warm breath on his cold hands in the hope of chasing away the chill. A dog barking in the town below caused him to glance in that direction and saved his life. He noticed the carriage's shadow cast on the blanket of snow and the silhouette of a figure behind him with a raised dagger in its hand. He spun around to face the hooded figure as a gust of wind blew the attacker's hood from his head. "Sebastian!"

The man smiled cruelly. "Merry Christmas, Butler." The dagger fell swiftly toward Butler's neck.

Suddenly, a dark form appeared and before Butler could blink, Sebastian was gone. He stared at the black clad figure who had replaced him and had no doubts who it was. "Shadow!"

Shadow raised a hand in greeting before moving to the front of the carriage and dropped into the seat beside Butler.

Totally shocked by what had just happened and the speed it had been carried out in, Butler stared at his unexpected travelling companion and watched as a hand reached for the black mask and pulled it off. A shake of the head released the long dark hair from its forced gathering.

"You're a woman!"

"I certainly am and a very pretty one at that," she held out a hand. "Hello, Butler. This greeting has been a long time coming."

Butler took the hand. "Um, hello, Shadow." He released her small black-gloved hand. "What are you doing here?"

"I thought that was obvious, saving your life."

"But why and where did you come from?"

"Why is difficult to answer, because I am not sure myself. Where I come from I can answer though. I have been following your exploits all day and climbed aboard the top of the carriage when you left Castle Drooge. I saw the rider approaching a couple of miles back and jumped off when he got close. I ran ahead and when I saw him climb onto the carriage and his intention was to kill you, I climbed a tree, jumped off when the carriage passed beneath and knocked him off while reclaiming my space atop the carriage."

Butler caught a whiff of lilac, recalling when he had smelt it last. "This is the second time you have saved my life. You killed Crakett!"

Shadow shrugged. "I'm not one for keeping score."

"I'm confused, why are you helping us? I thought you were working for Sebastian, just as Crakett was."

"Crakett Murdersin was not a good man. He had no honour and had killed many without a reason to do so other than it brought him enjoyment." She turned her head to look at Butler. "You, though, are a good man. I've been observing you and seen the way you look after the old man and the way he treats you."

"Ebenezer's alright, it's just his way." He turned to Shadow. "What do you mean *observing me*?"

"When Sebastian contacted me, and I accepted the job, I came to the Drooge estate to work out a plan. I spent a few days checking everything out and the people involved, including you, Ebenezer, Lurch, Sebastian and his men and the castle."

"You were in the manor?"

"I watched you all on and off for a for a few days. It's what I do before every job, get to know my enemy."

"You watched me *all* the time you were in the manor?"

"Not all the time, obviously, you are not that fascinating. I spent just long enough with each of you to get to know your habits and the sort of people you are."

"And what did you find out?"

"The result of my reconnaissance was that I kind of got to like the band of misfits that is you, Ebenezer, Lurch and even the foul breath Furtive. You are like a family who look out for each other. I like that, not having one of my own. As soon as I saw Sebastian I knew he wasn't a good man and one only a fool would trust. Because of these factors, I decided I wanted no part in his scheme, but when I learnt of the missing inheritance you were all trying to find, I'd thought I'd hang around to see if I could persuade some of it to come my way, so my time here wasn't a complete waste of effort."

"That's why you are here is it, to steal it?"

She shook her head. "No, you can keep it. I believed Sebastian might try something, so I decided I'd tag along for a while. Lucky for you I did. Though I don't know what he had planned for the others, I doubt it would have been anything good for their health. If I was in his position with Lurch, the wolf and Furtive guarding the treasure, I would have killed you and turned the carriage around gently so as not to alert those asleep inside, head back to the quarry and send it over the cliff. If everyone hadn't been killed, they would be injured and easy to finish off. I could then collect up the treasure, set fire to the carriage to burn the bodies and forget it ever happened."

"You really think Sebastian would really kill his own brother?"

"I'm certain he would, but you know him better than me, what do you think?"

Butler thought for a few moments. "Yes, I think he might, if the end result was he had the inheritance."

"That's probably why he suggested you take his carriage, so everyone could fit inside. I'm certain, even at that moment, he was forming a plan to get his hands on it."

Though Butler found it hard to accept, he did believe Sebastian was capable of such a terrible thing. "By the way, thanks for saving my life, twice."

"You are welcome, Butler."

"It doesn't seem fair that everyone has profited by this treasure hunt except you. I'm sure Ebenezer will pay the fee you arranged with Sebastian for not going through his plan to steal his painting, which I am certain you could have done at any time."

She pushed the offer away with a wave of her hand. "No need, I don't do it for the money. I like the adventure and the excitement. The thrill of not knowing what will happen next or if I will survive the encounter. Anyway, I have something better than money, I have some new friends if they'll have me."

Butler smiled. "I am sure we will. How old are you?"

"Though I don't see what that's got to do with anything, I am twenty-two years young."

"How and why did you become a thief and assassin?"

"That, Butler, is a story for another day." She smiled and put her arm through his. "So, where are we going?"

"I didn't realize *we* were going anywhere."

"I've got nothing else to do, so I thought I'd hang around for a bit."

"I suppose it is Christmas."

"Exactly, a time to spend with family and friends."

"Are you talking to yourself again, Butler?" shouted Ebenezer.

"Yes, Sir."

"Well stop it. It's annoying and I'm trying to get some sleep. And try to avoid the bumps; I get a shooting pain in my back with every jolt."

"Sorry, Sir, I'll try my best."

"And one more thing, Butler."

"Yes, Sir, what would that be?"

"Merry Christmas."

Butler smiled. "Merry Christmas, Sir."

After a few moments silence, Shadow asked, "Are you going to tell him what his brother tried to do?"

"I don't think so. I'm not sure how he will take it."

Butler steered the carriage onto the road that led to Havasham Hall and they sat in silence for a while.

"Do you think Sebastian is still alive?" Butler asked.

Shadow shrugged. "If he isn't that fall wouldn't have done him much good. I'd be surprised if he didn't break his neck or something."

"I can still hear you talking."

"Sorry, Sir, stopping now."

Sebastian slowly recovered consciousness and when he felt the pain shooting through his body he regretted doing so. Something pressed against his lips and forced something cold and disgusting into his mouth. He opened his eyes to stare into the face of a small grinning girl sitting on his pain-wracked chest. In one hand she held a spoon and in the other a bowl of grey runny goo. He watched the girl scoop out another disgusting spoonful of the lumpy grey slop and stab it toward his mouth, narrowly missing his eye. She maneuvered the spoon down his face leaving behind a trail of sticky grey slime until she forced it between his clamped lips and emptied its contents onto his tongue. After gagging the foul substance down, he tried to protest but found he couldn't speak or open his mouth more than a little. The little girl giggled sweetly at his mumbling sounds.

Though Sebastian had no idea where he was or who this strange child was, he suspected it might be Hell. The last thing he remembered was when he was about to kill Butler. Something slammed into him and he was flying through the air, which was followed by a very painful landing. He thought he remembered hearing a loud crack, but he couldn't be sure. He did though remember the world spinning and more pain. A stinging sensation as he rolled through something green and prickly. More pain followed by more pain, a crash of wood, more pain and then something struck his head and that was the last thing he remembered before waking up a moment ago.

A small dog barked nearby.

Sebastian tried to turn his head toward the sound but found it as immovable as his mouth and the rest of his body.

"Hello, Frisky, are you hungry?" enquired a man's voice.

The dog barked he was.

"Where's your bowl of pulverized offal?"

Sebastian stared at the bowl held by the little girl and knew exactly where it was. He watched helplessly when the spoon scooped out another helping.

"Oh, Katie, what are you doing? That's the dog's food."

Footsteps approached, and the bowl was taken from the girl's hands. A man's face, which he vaguely recognized, appeared and stared at him. Sebastian flicked his eyes frantically at the dog food laden spoon the small girl hid from her father, but the man failed to recognize the message.

"Gertrude, I think he's awake."

"About time, he's been out for three days."

A woman appeared and stared at him. If she wasn't a witch, she should be with her looks. "Well, his eyes are open, so I suppose that means his awake. Hello, Mr. Sebastian. Blink if you can hear me."

Sebastian blinked.

"You have had a nasty accident, Mr. Sebastian," said the vaguely familiar man "I went into the back garden to put out the garbage and found you there. You were in a right state, all shattered and broken, very similar to my fence you ruined when you smashed through it."

The witch woman shook her head. "You didn't look good, Sir, what with yer limbs pointing every which way. I thought yer were ready fer yer grave I did. We weren't sure whether to call the doctor or the undertaker."

The man took over. "So I dragged you indoors, and went and fetched them both. The doctor, who's more of a vet really, patched you up as best he could, which really won't win any awards or nothing, but it is what it is."

For some reason the woman smiled. "The doctor..."

"...vet, dear," corrected her husband.

"Oh, yeah, the vet said yer 'ave two broken legs, a broken arm, a dislocated shoulder, a dislocated jaw, probably a few cracked ribs—he weren't sure about that, but he wrapped yer chest in bandages anyway."

"He charges extra per foot of bandage," explained the man with a wink.

"You also rolled through a patch of particularly vicious nettles— we calls 'em *the devil's kiss* around 'ere we do, so all yer skin that weren't covered is a right mess of sores and blisters." She looked at her husband. "Is that everything, dear?"

The husband thought for a moment. It was painful to watch. "I think so, but the vet did say yer insides might not all be in the places they're meant to be after that tumble you had."

The woman grinned at Sebastian. "What this means is yer ain't gonner be able to move about much."

"Not at all, in fact," added the husband, a little too cheerily for Sebastian's liking.

Sebastian tried to talk again, but only a mumble passed his lips.

"Oh, yer won't be able to talk for a while yet, Sir," the man informed him. "Yer jaws all tied up, the vet left just enough slack to force some food in to keep yer alive."

"But don't you worry none about that, Mr. Sebastian, we'll look after yer, won't we dear?"

The man nodded enthusiastically. "It will be our pleasure. However long it takes before yer are back on your feet."

"Could be weeks, months even," said the woman, adding a large smile.

"And no need to worry about the cost either," said the man. "I found that money tucked in yer coat, so there's plenty to pay all yer bills while yer here. Food, lodging, the vet, creams and ointments fer yer skin, all those sorts of things. I also took some to pay for me fence yer destroyed; almost new it was so it weren't cheap. I also found some broken glass in yer pocket, right sparkly it was. Thought yer might have had a bottle of something to keep out the chill. Maybe that's how come yer fell off yer horse that was found wandering about outside the village. Took a too few many sips did yer, Mr. Sebastian? I ain't judging though, so don't think I am. Anyway, I threw the glass away. Didn't want yer cutting yerself, did we Gertie?"

"That's right. Safety first that's what I always say. I'm just about to cook dinner so yer'll be able to eat soon. We have succulent pork, roast potatoes and vegetables, but of course yer can't 'ave any of that."

"You have gruel, Mr. Sebastian, all yer can eat until yer jaw starts working again."

"Vet said that might be months also," added the woman, merrily.

"It don't taste right nice, but there's nothink we can do about that."

The woman screwed her face up in a grimace. "That be true, the dog won't go near it and that damn frisky thing will eat anything."

"But it has everything yer need to keep yer strong and breathing," the man added.

Sebastian felt like crying. This was worse than Hell.

"Look, Mr. Sebastian," said the man. "We are having some guests round for dinner tonight and I thought I'd better warn yer we'll be addressing you as uncle Seb, 'cause, um, yer ain't got a good reputation around these parts, but we ain't judging."

"No, we don't judge," agreed the woman. "Yer might be a right old angry miser that no one would waste their spit on if yer were on fire, but that don't mean nothing to us, does it dear?"

"Not at all," he said firmly. "Yer could be the devil himself..."

"Which some around these parts believe you are," said the woman.

"...and we would still show him the same kindness like we are yer."

"Well, I can't stand around here gossiping all day, dinner to prepare," declared the woman. A baby began crying. "Okay, Timmy, I'm coming."

"And don't worry about all your toilet workings, Mr. Sebastian. There's a hole in the chair you can let it drop through in ter a bucket and me and the wife will take turns with the liquid side of things. Just blink furiously when yer want to pee and one of us will grab a jug and aim yer willy in it."

The crying baby grew louder when the woman appeared with it in her arms. She laid the blanket she carried in the crook of Sebastian's well-bandaged and splinted arm, scrunched it up and laid the baby in it, which immediately stopped crying. "I hope you don't mind uncle Seb, but he loves it there he does, it's just the right shape ter make him feel all snugly and secure." Without waiting for the answer that would never arrive, she walked away.

"Yeah, I have things to do as well, so if yer want anything, Mr. Sebastian, just blink. It might take a while for us to notice, but likely sooner or later we will." He walked off whistling a merry tune. It was the family's best Christmas ever.

The dog strolled over and sniffed one of Sebastian's legs.

The girl smiled mischievously. Pulled the spoon out from around her back and plunged it toward his mouth. Unable to prevent her from doing so, Sebastian felt its foul contents slide down his throat and gagged.

The dog started rubbing itself friskily on his leg.

The baby squirmed, its face turned red and a satisfied smile followed a long, wet rasping squelch. The girl quickly jumped onto his cracked ribs and leapt to the floor. "Pooh, baby stinks, ma."

"I'm too busy to sort it now, I'll do it later," said the woman.

Sebastian wrinkled his nose as the smell began its first wave of attack. He glanced at the baby responsible; the frisky dog latched onto his leg, his broken, bandaged body and raised his eyes in despair. They focused on the painting on the wall directly opposite, a view impossible for him to turn away from. Shock and disgust fought for a place on the man's face. Sebastian now recognized the man he had thought familiar. It was Figgins, the tasteless art lover he had given the painting, the one the man had first thought was an elephant and which now assaulted his eyes.

Sebastian sobbed and inside screamed for a very long time.

Ben Hammott

EPILOGUE

REST AND
RELAXATION

Though **Agnes Havasham** had been surprised to discover Ebenezer knocking on her door, she had welcomed him and his odd band of companions inside. They had spent Christmas at Havasham Hall and stayed for a few days. Mrs. Havasham had one of her staff go to Drooge Manor to collect the horses from the stable and said she would have them cared for. Ebenezer entertained Mrs. Havasham in his unique style and she loved every moment. She said it was the best Christmas she had ever had. Though at first Butler, as a guest, found it strange and a little uncomfortable to be waited on by the staff, including Havasham's butler, he soon began to enjoy it. When it was time for them to leave, Mrs. Havasham was sorry to see them go and invited them all to come back next Christmas or whenever they liked. No one was sure if the invitation included Furtive, except for Furtive of course, but as they didn't plan on returning any time soon it wasn't really a problem.

Butler found an ideal house for Ebenezer in Devon. It overlooked the sea, had a nice garden and enough room for him and Lurch to live, as well as for a few guests. It also had a separate annex for the two staff Butler had arranged to take care of Ebenezer, a butler and a nurse. Though Ebenezer wasn't keen on the idea, he accepted it was necessary as Butler was insistent on leaving.

Shadow had disappeared shortly after leaving Havasham Hall without saying goodbye and they hadn't seen her since. Furtive, although he seemed reluctant to leave, had left a few days after Ebenezer had moved into his new home, with the promise he would check up on the old man from time to time.

Butler's parting was difficult and sad, but he knew it was the right decision for him if not for Ebenezer. He needed to get away and relax for a while and to work out what he wanted to do with the rest of his life now he had the funds to do so. Even knowing it would supply the means for him to leave, Ebenezer had been very generous with his share of the treasure and told him if he ever needed more all he had to do was ask. Butler had promised to keep in contact and booked passage on a steam ship heading for the Caribbean.

Though he had purchased some suitable clothing for the hot Caribbean climate, Butler remained dressed in his Butler's uniform, a habit he was finding hard to shake. There was no hurry, he told himself daily. He had only been here for two weeks and was willing to accept the change in his future gradually. He had taken off his shoes and socks, so he had made a start.

Shaded by an overhanging palm, he sipped his *Pina colada* cocktail, a tasty mixture of rum, pineapple and coconut milk, and gazed at the tranquil, turquoise sea. Gentle waves flowed and ebbed along the gently sloping shore of the deserted pale beach. He sighed with contentment as he readjusted his position on the padded sun-lounger. He doubted life could get better than it was at this very moment.

His nose wrinkled and fighting the desire to check the soles of his bare feet, he sighed.

"Hello, Butler. This place you've found is paradise. I bet it's not this nice in heaven and I wouldn't be surprised if God came here for a holiday."

Butler raised his sunglasses and turned his head. Furtive lounged on a chair, a cocktail in one hand and a smoking cigar in the other. "What are you doing here?"

"Thought yer might be lonesome all on yer own, so I thought to meself, Butler would be glad of the company, and so here I am. I can tell by the look on yer face it's a surprise. I do love surprises, don't you, mate?"

"Some are better than others." Butler then noticed the shorts and shirt Furtive wore. "Your clothes, which seem a few sizes too large for your scrawny form, look suspiciously like some of the ones I purchased soon after my arrival here."

Furtive glanced down at the white short sleeved shirt and blue shorts, flicked the wad of ash off and looked at Butler with a broad smile on his face. "There's a good reason for that."

Butler sighed.

"I have another surprise just as good as the last one..."

"You're not wearing any underpants."

"...No, not that, but you're right, I'm not." He squirmed in the chair and used a hand to release the shorts from the clutches of his sweaty buttocks.

Butler shivered.

Furtive's cigar pointed. "Look to your left."

Hesitantly, Butler turned to his left. His eyebrows leapt to his forehead for a better view. Butler's wide-open eyes thought they were in heaven as they roamed down the beautiful, bikini clad—black naturally—body of Shadow, until they were forced to focus on her face. "You look different," he said.

"Probably something to do with all this bare flesh on display and something you may have noticed when you ogled it just now."

"It was hard to miss," Butler admitted with a smile. "Are you also here to keep me company?"

"Nah, I'm just here for the sun. Dressed head to foot in black most of the time, it's nice to strip them off every so often and let the warm breeze caress my exquisite body."

"If the warm breeze gets bored, let me know and I'll jump in," offered Furtive, hopefully.

"The only thing you'll be jumping in around here is the deep blue ocean. It's bad enough having your eyes creeping over me without your hands adding to the discomfort."

"But Butler's eyes did the same."

"No, Butler's eyes have no hint of the creepiness yours are overflowing with; they admire the form and beauty that is me."

"Look, you two, I came here to relax in peace and quiet, so now you are here, let's all get along." Butler rested his head on the pillow, replaced the sunglasses over his eyes and let out a calming breath.

"What's the point of these tiny brollies they put in the drinks," Furtive asked, twirling one between his fingers.

"They stop the sun from melting your ice cubes so quickly," Butler told him.

"Oh, wow, that's amazing. What a brilliant idea." He looked at Butler. "Is there nothing you don't know?"

"If there is, it hasn't made itself known yet."

"It's wonderful here," stated Shadow.

"Paradise," said Furtive.

"Too damn crowded," groaned Butler.

Furtive giggled. "I love your sense of humour, Butler. See, you're having fun already."

Butler sighed. He was beginning to think only when he was dead would he truly be able to relax.

A few moments of quiet, that lasted longer than Butler had expected, was shattered by a commotion behind him.

"Careful, Lurch, you are spilling my cocktail."

"Sorry, Sir, but I can't see where I am putting my feet with you blocking my view."

"I don't want excuses, Lurch, just be careful. Drop me and you're fired."

"Is that a promise, Sir?" The hope was so obvious even Ebenezer detected it.

"No, it damn well isn't. Oh, look, there are the others." He raised a scrawny arm and waved. "Yahoo, I'm here."

Butler raised his sunglasses and peered at a small dark spot in the sea. Though he wasn't certain if it was a shark fin, he was willing to take a gamble and swim out to it in a distressed manner as possible and maybe even cut a vein to entice it over. The sun and the view of the shark that might have saved him from this torment, was abruptly blocked by something large and smiling.

"Hey ho, Butler," greeted Ebenezer.

"Hello, Butler, Sir," greeted Lurch.

Butler raised his eyes to look at Ebenezer held in Lurch's tree trunk arms. "Hello, Ebenezer. Hello, Lurch."

Ebenezer grinned. "Fancy seeing you here, just shows what a small world it is, eh?"

"Yes, Sir, that you should bump into me in the exact same place I told you I was coming to is an amazing coincidence and one I fathom to comprehend."

"Did you miss me?"

"Not for as long as I hoped, Sir."

"Still got yer dry sense of humour I see. Okay, Lurch, you can put me down now... in a chair!" he added quickly when he felt the man relax his grip.

Lurch laid Ebenezer gently on the lounger next to Butler and sat on the sand gazing out to sea.

Butler closed his eyes and waited for the next disturbance to shatter his relaxing holiday. It wasn't long coming.

A woman screamed.

Another quickly followed.

A loud howl filled the air.

Butler sighed.

A man's voice shouted, "It's a wolf!"

Lurch glanced toward the commotion with a broad smile on his face. "Wolfy's made some new friends." He whistled a whistle so shrill Butler thought his glass would shatter along with his ear drums.

Wolfy ran onto the beach, circled them all once, taking a wide berth around Furtive, bounded over to Butler, ran his tongue over his face dislodging his sunglasses before lying on the sand next to Lurch, his tail flapping back and forth flicked sand into the air and onto Butler's sun-lotion covered feet.

Butler looked at the wolf being stroked lovingly by Lurch. The beast certainly seemed happy and displayed none of its former viciousness.

"I was talking to the barman earlier," mentioned Furtive.

"Ah, that's explains the violent vomiting I heard," said Butler.

Furtive continued. "And he was telling me about all the pirate treasure that's rumoured to be hidden around these parts, including a lost treasure galleon belonging to Red Beard, the most feared pirate that ever plundered and murdered his way across the ocean. So, I got to thinking..."

"Never a good thing," sighed Butler.

"Why don't us lot go and search for some of this lost plunder. I know yer all don't need the money, but it'll be an adventure and we 'ave to do something fer fun."

"Something I was actually experiencing until a few moments ago," stated Butler.

"You'd soon get bored lounging about drinking fancy delicious cocktails in this paradise..."

"I'm sure I wouldn't, given the chance." Butler argued.

"We are the perfect team to go looking for lost pirate treasure. We have my excellent thieving skills, Butler's brains, Lurch's

- 315 -

considerable brawn, Eye Candy's impressive stealth..."

"I am not *eye candy*," complained Shadow.

Four pairs of eyes glanced at her in protest.

"Okay, so I am, guilty as charged milord, but I'd prefer to be addressed by my name."

"Okay, duly noted, *Shadow*. As I was saying, we are the perfect team to go looking for lost treasure."

Ebenezer coughed rather obviously. "You seem to have forgotten to mention the skills of a certain member of the team."

Furtive looked at the old man. "Well, you, Ebenezer, have um, ah." He glanced at the others desperately. "I could do with some help here."

None was immediately forthcoming until Lurch, surprisingly, spoke.

"Mr. Ebenezer is a lonely old man who realized too late a life without friends is not a life he wants to be part of. Look at us, we are all loners, but together we are a family, yes, dysfunctional at times, most definitely, but without Mr. Ebenezer none of us would have met or be here now. We need him as much as he needs us. I know I do. I have known Ebenezer longer than I have my own parents.

"Looking like I do and how children like to tease anything strange, my childhood was not a happy one. Though my parents did their best and loved me and were always kind, I could tell I wasn't the child they had longed for. When I was ten years old I wrote a note telling them I was going on an adventure and they weren't to worry, and I loved them. I then left home. I sometimes went back and hid in the trees on the hill overlooking their house, so I could watch. A year after I left they had another son, a normal boy and a year later another child, a girl. It made me happy to watch them laugh and play. I wanted nothing more than to run down the hill and share in this wonderful family life, but I didn't, because I knew I would ruin everything. They were better off without me. I turned away and never returned. I wandered across the country, avoiding the big towns as much as possible and found work on farms, or cutting wood for people and other odd jobs, but nothing that lasted long. People's pity doesn't last forever.

"One day I was walking along the road having no idea where I had come from or where I was going, when I heard the sound of horses behind me. I stepped to the side of the narrow road to let a carriage pass and it stopped a short way in front. A man, Ebenezer, poked his head out, looked at me for a few moments and then said, *'If you want work, climb aboard.'* I climbed aboard and have been with Ebenezer ever since. I have no idea why he stopped and offered me work, but I do know it wasn't because he had a job vacancy to fill.

"Why I told you that story is because Ebenezer and Mr. Butler are my family, and you

Furtive and Shadow are my friends. None of you judge me by how I look or because my brain is a bit slow. I feel normal around you all and I like that. So, perhaps Ebenezer's skill is in bringing likeminded people together. Though I don't rightly know if that is a skill, I do think it's important. I left my family once and I won't do so again. If Ebenezer is not on the team then nor am I, because I go where he goes and that's all I want to say."

There was silence for a moment.

Ebenezer wiped a tear from his eye and sniffed. "You ever say anything as heart-warming, kind and thoughtful as that again, Lurch, and you're fired."

"Is that a promise, Sir?"

"No, it damn well isn't."

"Obviously we are going to stay together, Lurch," reassured Butler. "But sometimes we have to part for a while to realize what we had and how much we miss it."

Ebenezer smiled warmly and felt another tear form.

"Back to my suggestion," prompted Furtive, totally unaware of anyone's emotional state, "What do yer think about hunting for this pirate treasure?"

"I'll give it some thought," Butler told him. He looked at Lurch's brightly coloured Hawaiian shirt and shorts, wondering where he had managed to find some large enough to fit his massive bulk. "Are you okay, Lurch?"

Lurch turned his head and smiled. "Yes, Butler, I am." He returned his gaze upon the ocean and stroked Wolfy's head.

Butler smiled. That was the first time the large man had called him by his name without the addition of a *Mr.* or a *Sir*.

"Oh, I'm okay as well, thanks for asking."

Butler hesitantly looked at his former employer. The small shorts he wore left too much wrinkled flesh on display to make one eager to set their eyes in his direction willingly. "I'm glad to hear it, Sir. You look good. A bit of colour on your pale, grey skin I believe."

"It's getting out of that damn dreary place and away from the bleak English weather that's done it. This sun is just what the doctor ordered."

"Um, no, not really, Sir. The doctor's words, as I recall, were, 'If your pale corpselike skin was ever exposed to bright sunlight for any length of time you'd burn like a vampire caught in daylight.'"

"Bah! Doctors think they know everything. Anyway, I brought protection. Lurch, where's my sun lotion?"

Lurch pulled a bottle from his shirt pocket and passed it to Ebenezer. "Would you like me to rub some on, Sir?"

"No, I wouldn't. Your hands are so rough it's like being scrubbed with a house brick. Shadow can do it."

"In your dreams, old man. There's no way I'm getting anywhere near that wrinkled corpse of yours, let alone touching it."

"Well, as there is no way I am letting sewer-mouth get too close to me..."

"Hey, that is the first time I have ever been glad to have foul breath, well actually, no, it's the second."

"An event that has yet to manifest itself to all others who have encountered it," said Butler.

Ebenezer continued as if the interruption hadn't happened. "...that only leaves you, Butler." He held out the bottle of lotion.

Butler's eyes desperately searched the ocean for any sign of the shark, but along with his chances of redemption, it too had disappeared. He sighed and took the bottle of lotion.

"I also have some cream for my bunions and that strange boil on one of my butt cheeks might need to be popped, but you can do that later, before we have dinner."

"Oh, what pleasure, Sir, my enjoyment never ends."

Unlike Butler's never-ending enjoyment, I am sorry to say this is **The End** of this story, but, lucky readers, please don't be disheartened, because it is not the last adventure Butler and co will have. They will soon return in a new misadventure. Please check my website **benhammottbooks.com** for updates and news of my other books.

I hope you enjoyed reading THE LOST INHERITENCE MYSTERY and you would consider doing me the great service of telling all your friends, including those on Facebook, tweet, write a review, (yes I know it's a pain, but it only needs to be a short one,) and spread the word any way you can. Authors starting down this publication road, of which I am one, need all the help and encouragement we can get and believe me, it is appreciated.

Thank you so much.

Ben Hammott

If you would like to be added to my mailing list to receive notifications of my new books, receive limited free advance review copies, send feedback or just to drop me a line, please contact me at:
benhammott@gmail.com

Your details will not be shared with anyone and can be removed at any time by contacting me via the above email address requesting your removal. Details of all the author's books can be found at
benhammottbooks.com

Printed in Great Britain
by Amazon